Praise for *Gabe Johnson Takes Over*

"A funny, uplifting, and rousing book that'll make readers think. In other words, it's a real gem."
—K. M. Walton, author of *Cracked* and *Empty*

"Told in the first-person voice that Geoff Herbach does so well, Gabe Johnson's account of his development of the 'leadership bone' is grand, touching, and hilarious."
—*Star Tribune*

"The funny, profane text embraces the idea that nobody is perfect. Gabe's character growth will satisfy any appetite. A funny popcorn read."
—*Kirkus Reviews*

"Framed as a transcript of events recounted by Gabe to his lawyer, Herbach's novel realistically addresses the difficulty of making major life changes and the empowerment of not feeling the need to blend in."
—*Publishers Weekly*

Praise for *Stupid Fast*

"Whip-smart and painfully self-aware, *Stupid Fast* is a funny and agonizing glimpse into the teenage brain."

—*Minneapolis Star Tribune*

"Felton's manic, repetitive voice and naive, trusting personality stand out in a field of dude lit populated with posturing tough guys and cynical know-it-alls."

—*Kirkus Reviews*

"In this struggling and often clueless teen, Herbach has created an endearing character coming to terms with his past and present in a small, well-defined Wisconsin town."

—*Booklist*

anything you want

Also by Geoff Herbach

Stupid Fast

Nothing Special

I'm with Stupid

Gabe Johnson Takes Over

anything you want

GEOFF HERBACH

sourcebooks
fire

Published by Sourcebooks Fire, an imprint of Sourcebooks, Inc.
P.O. Box 4410, Naperville, Illinois 60567-4410
(630) 961-3900
Fax: (630) 961-2168
www.sourcebooks.com

Library of Congress Cataloging-in-Publication data is on file with the publisher.

Printed and bound in the United States of America.
VP 10 9 8 7 6 5 4 3 2 1

In memory of my grandmother,
Yvonne Herbach, who proved optimism makes
for a better life.

CHAPTER 1

When did this start? Duh, dingus. Last spring.

Last spring I decided I was completely emotionally ready for her, so I asked Maggie Corrigan to prom, and she said, "Boom," and poked her finger into the middle of my chest.

I said, "Boom? That's good, right? That's a yes?" Maggie Corrigan is intense. She's wild and crazy and intense, and I had to be prepared for all that she can be.

We stood in the hall at school, leaned up against her locker as a bunch of freshmen, a total wad of screaming monkeys, ran by on their way to gym.

Maggie shouted, "Yeah, for sure, Taco! Boom!" She poked me again.

"What?" I shouted back because I couldn't hear over the freshmen.

"I totally want to go to prom with you!"

"Really?" I shouted back.

Then she grabbed my face and pulled my ears so my head came down to her face, and she French-kissed me right there in front of all those freshmen. She, like, kissed my ass off. My pants almost exploded from my body because she kissed me so hard.

She's spontaneous like that. I knew that then, but not like I know now. And you know what? It doesn't matter because I love her. I think I've loved Maggie Corrigan since before time. In a past life, I was probably the court clown, and she was probably the Crazy Queen of Holland. And I'm pretty sure we were doing it behind the king's back. If we weren't doing it, we were probably going on long naked walks in the forest, where we stroked unicorns and lay on the dewy moss to gaze upon the sky.

All the freshmen monkeys in the hall shouted stuff like, "Get a room," and, "More tongue." Freshmen are pretty funny. I've always liked them.

That day will go down in history for sure. I really needed Maggie Corrigan's energy and love right about then.

The year before Maggie kissed my ass off, Mom died. Six months after Mom died, Dad took a job driving trucks at a mine up north because we needed more money to float the boat. Two months after Dad left for the mine, Darius, my older brother, got a drunk-driving ticket, which he said he didn't deserve because he only had like two beers after work. It's just that his blood doesn't register alcohol like normal people's blood because it's a mix of O+ and A-, which is rare, so the cops didn't know what they were doing when they gave him the Breathalyzer. Okay, that didn't exactly make sense to me, but that's good old Darius! Anyway, he lost his Pepsi product delivery route and went to work at Captain Stabby's, this fish sandwich place, for about half the money. Dude smelled like fish twenty-four seven.

So things were crap, and I began to lose the pep in my cucumber. I was seriously beginning to think my mom was wrong about everything and maybe life really *is* terrible like Darius always says. But then I spent a few weeks following Maggie Corrigan around school and saw how she laughed until she fell on the floor, screamed when she got mad at her friends, cried when she was sad about the basketball team losing, and smiled so hard it looked like her face might break when I told her I liked her handwriting. After that I thought, *That's what Mom was talking about! Life is beautiful!* And so I summoned my good feelings and my optimism, and I asked Maggie to prom. A week later we were boyfriend and girlfriend and going at it in the hall between every class period.

Literally. Going at it!

Dr. Evans, our principal, had to bring us into the office to ask us to stop all the public displays of affection. (She called them PDAs.) Turned out our exhibits of love made some people uncomfortable—like those going through hard breakups or maybe the divorce of their parents.

Maggie and I tried, but we couldn't stop going at it. Sometimes to hide from people who might feel sad, we climbed into the costume loft behind the auditorium. Sometimes we took our clothes off, mostly so we could try on costumes but also because it was pretty great to get naked. Maggie would hang out up there in her underwear, pretending she had to find the perfect costume on the rack, but really, she just liked being naked with me.

Right on. I liked it too. See why I love Maggie?

At prom, we went nuts. I'm a good dancer, one of the best in my grade, and Maggie can slice the boards with the thoroughbreds due to her training as a cheerleader. At one point we were throwing each other in the air and ripping down streamers. At another point we did the double worm—Maggie on my back, holding on for her life, me on the floor, kicking and tucking like a tsunami wave. Nobody could believe we could dance like that. The only negative moment was when I ripped my pants jumping off the DJ's table to land a split. Everybody cheered and high-fived me, but I lost the deposit on my tux, which made Darius mad because we couldn't afford any more disasters.

Still, prom was amazing. After the dance, Maggie

and I climbed a firefighter tower out by Belmont. We totally got naked up there too.

I was on the hottest of all hot streaks possible. In track I ran faster than I ever had before and earned the second alternate spot on the four-by-four hundred relay team, which meant I got to go to La Crosse for the state track meet just in case those two guys got injured. We stayed in a hotel. I had to share a bed with Brad Schwartz, but it was a king-size (which was huge), so we didn't accidentally wake up spooning with our hands in our muffins. And I had the greatest breakfast of all time. Have you ever had a continental breakfast? They had one at the hotel. I ate six little boxes of Froot Loops, fourteen pieces of bacon, three cinnamon buns, and eight cups of coffee with these little blue vanilla creamers that tasted like milk mixed with frosting. What a cornucopia!

Last spring will likely go down as the greatest of my life.

And that led to summer, which was even better because Brad Schwartz's dad manages—wait for it—the swimming pool! And he hired me to be the towel boy and the janitor. During the day, I emptied the baskets of used towels and restocked the shelves with fresh ones in the men's locker room. Working inside was good because I would get pretty hot in the sun. Then when I worked at night, I got to be in the cool air while I cleaned up candy wrappers and lost socks from around the kiddie pool. One time I found a Barbie watch, and nobody claimed it, so Mr. Schwartz said I could keep it. I tried to give it to Maggie, but she said, "I'm not an eight-year-old!" so I wore it around instead. I don't know why she didn't like it. You can get it wet and it still tells time.

Speaking of Maggie, she would come to the pool at night to see me, and she'd wear a bikini, which showed off all her extreme and natural beauty. And she'd do flips off the diving boards, even the high one.

Then when my shift was done, we'd go streaking in Smith Park. I felt like a baby deer jumping over the ditches and fallen trees. Maggie's quite a bit faster than me. The girl can fly! She should have gone out for track, except her cheerleading duties would've gotten in the way.

Oh, cheerleading. Maggie was very serious about cheerleading. So it seemed to make sense when in August, after our summer of love, she started to run out of time to hang with me. Between her work at Dairy Queen and the start of fall practice, Maggie was *so spent*. That's what she told me. "I wish I could see you tonight, Taco, but I'm *so spent*."

I believed her, but I still wanted to see her. I figured it was up to me to make that happen, so I ran across

Bluffton at midnight, hiding in the shadows and dodging night squirrels. When I got to her old Victorian house near the college, I'd climb the trellis on its side and slide in through her bedroom window.

Maggie was psyched to see me. But two of her sisters, younger Missy and older Mary, also shared her room, so I couldn't stay very long. They didn't like me sliding in. In fact, they'd get seriously pissed when I'd wake them up by falling on the floor or stepping on their beds. It was so dark, I couldn't see where I was going. Sometimes Maggie and Missy and Mary would get in fights because those sisters got so mad about me being in the house, sitting on their pillows or whatnot.

Maggie's parents didn't like me either, which is too bad because I totally liked them. Maggie's mom would scream at me when she caught me in her house in the middle of the night. I could totally see where Maggie got her intensity! Her mom would sort of go crazy.

In fact, it got so bad over there that Mr. Corrigan chased me down in the Piggly Wiggly (that's a grocery store) and grabbed me by my jean jacket collar and nearly threw me into a bunch of mayonnaise jars because he was so mad.

"Taco! Not again! We've been as patient as we can be, young man. We've warned you again and again. If

7

you scale our home one more time, you'll find yourself behind bars!" he shouted.

Everybody in the store looked on like they were watching TV. Except instead of watching *Cops* or some show about bounty hunters, they were watching me and Mr. Corrigan.

That was tough. I love Mr. Corrigan! He has a beard, and all his jackets have leather patches on their elbows. Man, I love his jackets. He's an English professor. When I picked up Maggie for prom back in the spring, Maggie's mom was going through a list of rules for us while we were at the dance, but Mr. Corrigan told her not to worry so much. He said, "Read your Shakespeare. Sometimes the fool's the smartest man in the kingdom." He really is a fantastic guy.

But he wasn't happy that night at the Piggly Wiggly. Not at all. I didn't want him to be so upset, so I agreed I wouldn't scale their home ever again. I crossed my fingers behind my back so God wouldn't get mad at me for lying. Because you see, I absolutely had to tell Maggie that I couldn't sneak over anymore and that we'd have to find a different way to see each other. She absolutely had to hear the news from me before she heard it from someone else, so I snuck back later that same night.

This time the Corrigans were ready for me though.

I got about halfway up the trellis when a big floodlight turned on and an alarm started blaring. If Mr. Corrigan had told me there was an alarm, I wouldn't have climbed the side of the house. I might have dug a tunnel into the basement or parachuted onto the roof, but I wouldn't have lost my grip and fallen into Mrs. Corrigan's raised-bed tomato garden. I had the wind knocked out of me so hard, I thought I was a dead boy.

Five minutes later all those Corrigan girls—Missy, Mary, Misha, Molly, and Maggie—were outside in their white nightgowns. They were crying, and Mr. Corrigan was on his horn, calling for an ambulance because a perpetrator (me) was lying on their lawn. Surprisingly (especially given how strict she can be), Mrs. Corrigan was nice.

"Don't you move an inch," she said.

I wanted to get up because it was uncomfortable having those tomatoes under my back, but she said, "If you move your head, you might permanently injure your spinal cord, and I don't want your father to sue us for this idiocy."

The ambulance came, and a bunch of neighbors showed up to see what was happening. After the medics immobilized my neck, I waved at the people I knew and threw Maggie a few kisses too. Maggie wanted to ride in the ambulance, but her parents wouldn't let her. Mrs. Corrigan rode in the back with me. I couldn't see her very well because of the neck brace, but it looked like she held her head in her hands the whole ride. Mr. Corrigan drove Mary and Maggie in his car. Missy had to stay home to watch Misha and Molly because those girls were pretty young and could get injured or kidnapped if left unattended.

I was really pleased to find Dr. Steidinger in the emergency room. He's my doc! He's almost ninety-seven years old, so he's quite wise. He brought me into this world, so I trust him with my life.

"Where does it hurt, Taco?" he asked.

"I popped both my lungs," I said.

He put his cold stethoscope on my chest and listened to me breathe.

"Your lungs aren't popped. They're pumping quite nicely. Any other pain?"

"My head. I might be hemorrhaging upstairs."

He shined a little flashlight into my eyeballs.

"No sign of asymmetric dilation. Why don't you sit up?"

This is when the full extent of my injuries became known. When I sat up, my butt fired pain all through my nether world and out my toes.

I screamed.

"Roll over," Dr. Steidinger said.

I turned and the pain got even worse.

"Lie flat on your belly. I'm going to pull down your trousers now."

"Careful! Careful!" I shouted.

"Hm. We'd better get X-rays."

"What?" I cried. "What?"

Here's the what-what. I broke my coccyx by falling off the Corrigans' house! The coccyx is the tailbone, but I was worried people wouldn't understand my truth if I told them about my tail, so I asked Dr. Steidinger if we could agree to call my injury a broken butt. We agreed to disagree on the matter, which I understood because Dr. Steidinger has a reputation to protect. I do too.

So there I was at the dawn of the new school year, which was to be my junior year at Bluffton High School, and I had a broken butt. What of football? I was slated to be the fourth-string running back! What of gym class and all the badminton birdies I might whack? What of sitting in biology or English or social studies or, most importantly, calc—the hardest class in the whole school? Unfortunately for yours truly, my butt was crushed and unable to function the way a junior's butt should.

In fact, I had to miss the first two weeks of school because it hurt so much to move. And then I had to sit on an inflatable doughnut to keep my coccyx from contact with hard surfaces. No football. No gym. Inflatable doughnut.

You might think my hot streak had ended, right? No way. If anything, life got even better. Well, maybe not in hindsight, which is twenty-twenty.

No, really, actually, I wouldn't change anything.

CHAPTER 2

When Mom was a nurse and Dad drove trucks for Fendall, we were pretty much the richest people in town—or at least we were close to the richest. We had this kick-ass split-level over by Westview Elementary. I always thought of that house as a super fly mullet. You enter the front door and there're stairs that go up and stairs that go down. You go up for the business. You go down for the party. Darius and I had our bedrooms on the lower level. We also had a pool table that you could make into a Ping-Pong table and an Xbox that Darius played until his eyeballs turned into bloody discs of doom. Darius always had buddies over, and I would fire Ping-Pong balls out of my mouth at their heads until they chased me and wrestled me to the ground or whatever.

Take away Mom (because she died) and her nursing job, take away Dad's job at Fendall and send him up to drive a dump truck, like, ten thousand miles away from Bluffton, and you get a different, cheaper house—a rental on the east side of town right by the high school.

It was a prefab. That means the house was actually built in some factory and then stuck on a truck and delivered to our yard in one piece! Crazy!

In order to fit on the truck, the house was a lot smaller than the mullet house, but pretty much Darius and I were the only ones living there, so downsizing didn't mean downspacing. In fact, my bedroom was huge. It was the master suite! It had its own toilet.

I'm not sure why I got the big bedroom and Darius took the basement, except he's always liked basements. Really, Darius should've slept wherever he wanted because of all he did for me. He dropped out of tech school to work so I could keep being a normal kid. That's what he promised Mom he'd do as she pulled her last breaths. Take care of me. Stop me from becoming an adult too soon. When I got the job at the pool, he called up Mr. Schwartz to make sure the job ended before school started because he didn't want me working during the school year. He also put all my money away for college instead of letting me spend it. Darius really took his Taco caretaking seriously. He really tried at times, even though he's messed up.

Any-hoo.

The first two weeks of September were amazing. Because of my broken butt, I couldn't really walk, so I had to stay home from school.

Dad came down from the mine for Labor Day weekend, and he bought me ten frozen pizzas and a loaf of bread and some peanut butter I could keep on my side table. He made Darius promise he'd cook me some of the pizzas. Darius said he would, but he only did it once. After work at Captain Stabby's, he didn't have the energy. (He also smelled like a fish, and my preference is to have my pizza smell and taste like pizza, not Darius.) No problem! Dad hung out at home for like a full four hours that weekend, which was a record since he moved up north, so that was awesome.

As for school, Brad Schwartz, the largest pal of my life, delivered my homework every day. He was an old pro at doing this kind of work. During Mom's last three weeks of life, he and Akilesh Sharma were at the house all the time, helping me stay on top of the ocean of school-work. Both back in the days of cancer and during my coccyx troubles, Brad talked me through my lessons. He's one of the top ten or so smartest dudes in the state of Wisconsin (right up there with Sharma), so I picked up everything I needed to know, except for calc, which I didn't really get.

During this initial coccyx rehab, I spent more time doing homework and reading books than I ever had before, and it was really interesting. If you haven't read

Lord of the Flies, I highly suggest you do. Even to this day, more than eight months after I read that book, I still have dreams about little dudes in underpants stabbing me with sticks. The book also made me want to eat a bunch of ham because the stick dudes kill pigs and eat them. I was so lucky that the pizzas Dad bought had Canadian bacon.

And I haven't even mentioned the most intriguing development of my two weeks of bed recovery. Every day when Maggie Corrigan finished cheerleading practice, she came over to provide comfort and love.

Generally speaking, her parents hadn't let her spend time at my house because of the lack of parental supervision. (I once told Mrs. Corrigan that Mom's ghost watched over me and that she kept Maggie safe too, but Mrs. Corrigan's didn't think that was the same.) It didn't really matter anyway because Dad had barred me from having any female company at the house. "If I hear a peep about girls coming over to party, I'll move your ass up to the mine and you'll go to work," Dad said.

But things changed with the broken butt. First, the Corrigans let Maggie come over. They had almost killed me with their alarm, and they felt guilty. Second, I decided to break Dad's rule about no female visitors because my butt hurt and I couldn't think straight, which seemed like a good excuse. Besides, Dad never checked on me anyway, so how could he hear a peep? Thirdly, Maggie's parents had actually been trying to force her to break up with me before I broke my butt, so I had to let Maggie in my bedroom as much as possible!

How did I find out about the forced breakup? Maggie confessed.

On Wednesday during the first week of school, Maggie showed up after cheerleading and lay down on my bed next to me and cried. She sobbed. Her tears soaked all the sheets and pillows. When she feels something, it's for real.

"What's happening, Maggie?" I asked.

"This is my fault. You broke your butt because of me," she cried.

"I was the one who fell. That's not your bad."

"Do you know why you had to climb our house?" she whispered.

I had to think for a second. "Because between shooting the soft serve at Dairy Queen and your cheerleading practice, you didn't have time to see me, so I had to make midnight visits."

"No, it's because I couldn't stand up to Mom and Dad," Maggie cried. "They told me not to see you anymore."

This news came as quite a shock, dingus. The

Corrigans didn't want Maggie seeing me at all? Not just when I broke into their house? Why?

While I hadn't completely understood why they got so upset about me visiting at midnight, in some ways it seemed reasonable. Sleep is an important part of growing up with a healthy mind and strong bones, and my forced entry disturbed their daughters' sleep. But the fact they wanted me and Maggie completely broken up made *zero* sense.

"Is there some reason they don't like me?" I asked. "I always try to give them hugs and high-fives when I see them."

"They think we're impulsive and that we're doing it all the time, and they don't want me to be doing it because I'm too young."

"Aha!" I shouted. "But we aren't doing it," I said. "I never asked you to do it. Even though I want to do it, I also don't want to do it. Because if I do it, then I'll have already done it, and I want to do it when the time is right."

Maggie stopped crying and sat up. "You don't want to do it?"

"I do, but I don't."

"I want to do it," Maggie said.

"You do?" I asked.

"Yeah, man. We're great together. We laugh all the time, and you're sweet. We're the perfect couple, and I think doing it would be perfect, right? Are you saying you won't do it?" Maggie asked.

I thought, but I couldn't really think. "I said no such thing," I replied.

"Then why haven't we done it? Am I not good enough for you?"

"You're the best. You're the greatest ever."

"I know. That's how I feel about you. So we should do it," Maggie said.

"We should?" I asked. I felt so dizzy, dingus! Clearly Maggie loved me!

"Let's do it this weekend," she said. "Or maybe next week."

I had lost my breath. "Here? In my bed?"

Maggie rolled over and kissed me so long and hard that my coccyx hurt.

The whole next day, Thursday, I did nothing but think about doing it. Even when I fell asleep, my dreams were filled with naked Maggie and me always just about to do it. The thing is that if I really thought about it (which was hard because Maggie Corrigan is the love of my universe and I'm a junkie for her), I didn't think I wanted to do it. Not that I didn't want to do it, if you know what I mean. These dreams weren't super sexy dreams. They were highly stressful.

My mom, right before she died, grabbed me by my hands (which took more strength than I thought she had) and told me all these things she thought I needed to know for the future, things that Dad wouldn't tell me. Although Dad is an okay guy, he isn't very courageous and doesn't like to talk to me.

She said, "Your dad isn't going to have enough money. He is terrible with money, and I didn't plan for this. I'm so sorry. Your dad tries his best, but you have Darius. He'll take care of you even if your father can't."

She said, "Don't believe your brother when he says mean things. Darius has a lion's heart, but he was born angry, probably from something that happened in a past life. He has to work that out for himself. Don't believe his negativity, you understand? But when he tells you to stop picking your nose in the car because other people can see you, believe that. It's true. Don't do that."

She then said, "You have so much love inside you, Taco. You have so much to offer the right girl. Don't give away that love when you're too young. Wait until you find the right girl and you're both mature enough to know what a gem you have in each other, and then your love will be protected like it should be."

She said, "You were born special. You were born to do this family proud. You make *me* proud, Taco."

She said, "Today is the best day of your life. So is tomorrow and the next day and the next day and the next. No matter what happens, every day you have is the best day of your life."

"Today is the best day of my life," I said, though it didn't feel that way.

"Darius is going to help you," Mom whispered. "He hurts, but remember, he has a lion's heart. And you're brothers. You're family."

Mom squeezed my hands a little tighter and said she was going to miss me, but she was excited to see what was on the other side. Then she smiled, and the skin around her eyes crinkled, which made her look like a sad bald elf. And then she told me I was a good boy. Like an hour later, she was gone.

My mom was a super genius and also a mystical spirit goddess. She's either a nice ghost now that watches over me or she's a flying baby who lives in Tibet. (I've had both dreams, so I don't know which reality is the truth. Maybe both? I meditate and talk to both the ghost and the baby at times.) In any case, I listened to the lady. Even during the great sadness after she died, after we left the mullet house and Dad went north and Darius was arrested, I repeated what she said to me again and again. *Today is the best day of my life and so is tomorrow.*

But this thing with Maggie Corrigan really threw me off. I wasn't sure if Maggie was mature enough to treat me like the gem I am. I just knew what I still know. I love Maggie Corrigan.

While I was lying in bed, I tried to figure out if Maggie Corrigan, whom I love and whom I figured would one day be my wife, was mature enough to treat me like the gem I am.

On the positive side of this chart were the following: She's hot. She's daring. She's fast. She's a good jumper. She's a good wrestler. She's a good driver, although she doesn't like to drive. She is more fun than Ping-Pong and bowling combined. She's filled with joy that makes the world glow. Her sadness opens a black hole in the fabric of time and space, but it closes as soon as she is happy again. And she is happy a lot of the time. She's happy when she's naked, in a bikini, in a wool hat, and in snow boots. She is happy in whatever she wears because she is happy with herself, except when she's sad or mad, which does happen. And most importantly, she is happy when she is with me. She loves me.

On the negative side of this chart were the following: Her parents don't think she's old enough to do it. Her parents don't want us to be together, which is why I had to climb their house to see her, which is why I broke my butt.

Maggie's positives clearly outweighed her negatives, but I had the nagging feeling that the negatives affected her ability to treat me like the gem I am. I was very confused. I read a bit of *The Fellowship of the Ring* to get my mind off the matter.

Around 2:00 p.m., Darius woke up, and he came upstairs to get some non-Stabby's food in his gut before he headed off to the Captain's for his fish shift. I called for him to visit me in my master suite bedroom. It took him a few minutes, but after I yelled and yelled, he opened the door.

"What? What the hell, Taco?"

"Do you think Maggie Corrigan treats me like the gem I am?" I asked.

"Are you kidding me?"

"No. What do you think?"

"Why are you asking?" Darius asked.

"Because she wants to do it—you know, *do it*—but I need to be sure she's completely ready before I agree."

Darius stared at me for a moment. Then he said, "No, absolutely not. Don't do it. She doesn't love you."

"Well, sure she does," I said.

"No. How would you even know?"

"I just do. We are definitely in love, Darius."

Darius glared at me for a moment. Then he shrugged. "You're stupid," he said. "She doesn't love you." He turned and walked down the hall.

Darius used to be in love, but this girl, Kayla Kronstadt, whom he dated all through high school and our mom getting sick and Dad leaving, broke up with him when he got his drunk-driving ticket. Darius said it was because he couldn't drive her places anymore after he lost his license. But she didn't get back together with him when he started driving again. Of course, he doesn't always make great decisions, and he's kind of a jerk sometimes. And he's drunk a lot, so maybe that all has something to do with it. Also, he's broken inside.

Anyway, I wasn't sure what Darius's advice had been. He told me I was stupid. But I didn't ask him if I was stupid or not. He also said Maggie didn't love me, which clearly wasn't the case. Mom said that I shouldn't listen to Darius when he said mean things, and wasn't he being mean by calling me stupid and not loved?

Whatever. I got very quiet. I meditated to try to communicate with Mom's ghost. I heard nothing. I tried to summon the Tibet baby that I dream about that might be Mom. I couldn't do it. And I thought, *Maybe that's your answer. Nothing!*

Right? Nothing! Do nothing!

Because honestly, while I was sure Maggie loved me, I wasn't sure she could yet love me like the gem I am. *That settles it!*

Sorry, lady pal! No. Doing. It.

I felt very good about this decision, very smart and mature.

After school, Brad Schwartz came over, and we had a good talk about democracy. The lessons he brought home in both English and social studies had to do with democracy. Using the little boys in their underpants killing one another with sticks and rocks from *Lord of the Flies*, Brad tried to convince me that democracy is doomed to fail.

"We have a base nature," he said. "We're more animal than creatures of reason."

"You're wrong!" I said. "Those kids on the island are just kids. They don't have the maturity to make good choices. If they were a couple years older, like our age, they wouldn't have crushed one another's skulls with rocks. They'd have figured out democracy—no problem."

Brad rolled his yes. "Have you seen the cafeteria without a lunch monitor? You're delusional, Taco."

"No, I'm not," I said.

He shrugged and left.

Later when Maggie Corrigan showed up after

cheerleading practice, she said all she could think about was my body.

"This body?" I asked.

She nodded. Then she gently removed my bear slippers and my pajama pants, careful not to hurt my coccyx, and she carefully put her naked knees on either side of my hips and leaned over. As she breathed in my ear, she whispered, "I love you so much, man." That was when I decided we should definitely do it.

And we did! It kind of hurt Maggie, which made me worried, but she said she was okay. We fell asleep. Then—wait for it—we did it again!

It was great! I couldn't wait for my broken butt to heal so I could actually move while we were doing it! I mean, so great! Oh my God, I love Maggie. I'm a junkie for her for real!

But here's the deal, dingus: Life begets life.

I read that in a biology textbook. Or maybe it was the Bible?

I can't remember.

CHAPTER 3

For the rest of my broken butt convalescence, Maggie came over to the suite after every cheerleading practice. Good times! We were celebrating our love. Of course, sex is sex even if you call it a celebration.

And then my coccyx was ready to attend school!

It was great to get back. Everybody was so happy to see me. Jocks, jerks, dweebs, dinks, doinks, dickheads, burners, boners, geeks, brats, preps, and trench coat loners all high-fived and hugged me that first day. "It's like the school lost its beating heart," Ms. Tindall said. I knew she was right. Ms. Tindall is the health teacher. She has access to academic articles and school transcripts and understands a school's culture. She knows the what-what.

I couldn't play football, of course. There weren't football pants big enough to fit around my inflatable doughnut, which would protect my healing coccyx from offending helmets. That didn't mean I couldn't be involved though. I became the best equipment manager and water boy Bluffton High School has ever known. Coach

Johnson has a son who played at Iowa, and he coached a kid who got a full ride to Stanford as well as a bunch of other guys who play at small colleges. He actually said as much. "Son, I appreciate how far up my ass you are. You're doing a fine job, but could you take a step back?"

"Yes, sir. Yes, sir!" I said and saluted him.

During games, I got to hand out Gatorade on the sideline and cheer, which meant I was close to Maggie and her kicking legs and her jumping booty and her total love. She'd blow kisses at me and lick her fingers like she was eating a sexy ice cream cone. Being water boy also meant I got to be in the locker room for Coach Johnson's inspiring pregame, halftime, and postgame speeches.

But Maggie was changing just like the seasons.

It was October, at a game in the hills of Richland Center, when I first noticed Maggie's changing moods. I came limping out on the field after halftime just in time to see Maggie refuse to climb to the top of the cheerleader pyramid. Without Maggie, they were a cheerleader trapezoid, which wasn't impressive at all. She stood behind the tower of her teammates with her arms crossed while the other girls shouted at her. She shouted back, sort of crying, her face the color of a cherry slushy.

"What's wrong?" I shouted. I ass-hobbled over to her. The cheerleader trapezoid collapsed to the ground.

She just shook her head at me, tears in her eyes.

"Seriously. What's wrong, Maggie?" I put my hand on her shoulder.

"My boobs hurt. I can't jump anymore. They ache," she whispered.

"Oh?" I said. "Should I ice them down when we get back to the suite?" That's what guys on the football team do when a body part aches.

"Okay," she said.

"Okay," I said. She nodded, but I don't even think she heard my words. Her eyes looked far away, even beyond the stands, like deep into the hills and past the trees and deer and cliffs, off into the deepest darkness of Wisconsin.

"Okay," I whispered. Then the football team came back on the field, and I cheered and cheered because I loved football.

After the game Maggie said her boobs were fine. I didn't have to ice anything. She was very uncomfortable and sweaty and weird though. She was also huggy, like she didn't want to let go of me, which I liked, but it was pretty out of the norm for her. Usually Maggie stayed at the suite long enough for us to hang out and do it. Then she'd walk home by like ten thirty. But that night she stayed until 1:00 a.m., and we just talked and talked and hugged until her dad showed up and asked if she needed a ride home. Mr. Corrigan's face was all gray, and there were these big circles under his eyes. It looked like he wasn't too pleased to be awake, but he was wearing one of his jackets with the elbow patches anyway. Man, is that guy classy.

Then Maggie went quiet on me for the weekend.

She spent Saturday and Sunday at her big house, doing yard work and cleaning the basement and the attic and painting her and Mary and Missy's bedroom. (Apparently I'd scuffed up the walls with my shoes during the summer.) So I didn't get to see her.

I didn't get a glimpse of her again until Sunday night, when I visited her at Dairy Queen, because I figured she wouldn't mind the company there.

But at Dairy Queen she hissed at me. "You! You did this!"

"What?"

She pulled me into the men's bathroom and told me her boobs hurt and asked me if I had any idea what that might mean. I told her I had no idea. Then she glared at me and called me a child.

So I said, "I'm your boyfriend. I'll take care of you. How about you come over after work, and we'll ice your boobs so they don't ache?"

Maggie turned all cherry-slushy face again and threw me out of the store. I didn't want to leave, but she threatened to call the police—kind of like her mom might do. So I limped home and got a big headache to go with my butt ache and my heartache because I was so confused.

And then I got even more confused. Two hours later she showed up at my house in her family's fantastic Subaru wagon and acted like nothing had happened at the Dairy Queen.

"What was that about, Maggie?" I asked, standing at the door.

"Oh, I don't know. You were just being annoying."

"You would call the cops on me for being annoying?"

She grabbed my ears and pulled me to her lips. "I'm sorry. I love you. Let's just do it," she whispered. So we did, and then she cried great heaving sobs.

"What's wrong?" I cried.

"It's okay. I don't know. I'm sorry. I'd better go," she said between sobs. Then she left!

After that she barely talked to me for several days, which made me sick to my stomach.

Then on Thursday after school, I had a short football practice. It was the day before a game, so all I did was pack up the first-aid kit. Maggie's cheerleading was canceled too, and we ran into each other outside the gym. She said, "Let's go get naked."

I was all like, "Oh yeah? Really? Maybe…if you think you won't cry for no apparent reason and then leave me and not answer my phone calls."

"Ha-ha!" she said like I was making a joke, which I wasn't. "Let's go!"

When we got back to the suite though, she couldn't do anything but take pees. She went like twenty-five times until she squealed, "Spotting! Maybe I'm okay?" Then she left again.

I didn't have a laptop or a smartphone or even a cell phone. Darius had one, but he couldn't afford two, so I had to use the landline. But we did have the Internet. It was hooked up to my mom's old desktop, which sat on our kitchen table so that both Darius and I had access to it.

After Maggie left, I sat down at the computer and looked up hurting boobs and spotting, which I found out often have their root cause in the menstrual cycle. Maggie was having her "little friend," which is what she called her period. Suddenly her crazy behavior made sense.

The next day at school, I hugged her. "Of course your boobs hurt, and you're spotting, lady pal. You've got your little friend."

Maggie hit me. "You don't know shit from Shinola."

I figured she might be right. I might not know shit from Shinola because I didn't know what Shinola was. But Maggie didn't seem like she was in the mood to hear that, even if I was agreeing with her.

That night we had a home game against Lancaster. Maggie was totally normal. She jumped and cheered and laughed while our team got our asses handed to us in the first half. At halftime she climbed to the top of the cheerleader pyramid. And right before the start of the third quarter, right before we received the kickoff, Maggie kissed me square on the lips in front of everyone.

"I want you so bad!" she told me. But after the game, she called her mom to pick her up and take her home from the stadium. She said she was having cramps.

Shit from Shinola?

Later, I sat in my dark kitchen at mom's old computer. I looked up shit from Shinola. It turns out Shinola is shoe polish that was very popular during World War II. I began to wonder if maybe a World War II ghost had invaded Maggie, and maybe that's why her boobs hurt and why she had to pee all the time. I'd heard about similar cases on the TV show *Ghost Adventures*, which Darius likes to watch sometimes.

Even later that night, I sat on my doughnut on the

couch in the living room and read a biography of Thomas Jefferson, which had been assigned for English. Jefferson, it turns out, was a pretty crazy man, so I enjoyed myself, forgetting about the haunting of Maggie Corrigan's boobs.

About 10:00 p.m., the front door opened, and the smell of tainted fish and stale beer enveloped me as Darius stomped in, pulled off his fish clothes, and complained about the grease that was giving him zits.

"Did you drink beer and then drive?" I asked.

"Not your business," he said before microwaving some nachos.

When he finally settled down on the couch to eat, I asked, "Have you ever known anybody who's been possessed by a spirit or maybe a devil?"

"What? No." Darius stuffed a bunch of chips in his face.

"Maggie's possessed, I'm pretty sure," I said. "One minute she says she loves me so much, but like a minute later she's screaming at me because I'm annoying—like so annoying that she feels the need to call the cops. And her boobs hurt. They didn't hurt when we first started dating. And she has to pee a lot. And she cries for no reason."

Darius stared at me. He said quietly, "That's funny."

"You wouldn't think it was funny if you saw it happening," I said.

Darius blinked. He held chips in both his hands (unwashed hands, I'm sure, so the chips surely tasted like fish). He blinked some more but didn't move. He didn't jam those chips in his mouth. He just stared and blinked.

"What?" I asked.

"I can hear what you do," Darius said very quietly.

"What do I do?" Fear bloomed in my heart because now Darius seemed haunted too. "What do you mean?"

"You do it. You and Maggie Corrigan do it all the time. Again and again and again," he said.

"Right. We like to celebrate our love," I said.

"Jesus Christ, Taco. Is she on birth control?" he asked.

"No." I laughed. "Why would she be?" As I tend to be delusional but not totally stupid, I began to think.

"Oh shit. Are you using condoms?" he asked.

"No. We're not serious about it, okay? We're just having fun." Then I started to really think because that sounded like a very, very dumb statement.

"Oh shit, Taco," Darius said.

"What? What are you saying?" Oh balls, dingus! I knew what he was saying!

Darius sat forward, so a couple nachos fell on the floor. "I'm supposed to be the dumb one, Taco. I'm supposed to be the one who doesn't understand causes and consequences—the one Mom said needs to take a big breath before I act because I'm liable to fall off a damn cliff without noticing."

"Well, you do have a certain history," I said.

"Haven't you taken health class?"

"I'm in health two this year," I said. "Ms. Tindall thinks I'm smart."

"First thing we learned about in my class was pregnancy and how you get pregnant. You don't have to want to get pregnant to get pregnant, dumb ass."

"I know that," I said. But what started to play on repeat in my mind was, "Oh shit. Oh shit. Oh shit."

"Is your girlfriend trying to get pregnant?" Darius asked.

"I don't know. I don't think so."

"You idiot!"

"I know," I whispered.

Oh, dingus, did I know. In health class during freshman year, we learned about sperms and eggs and... oh shit. I knew it all. And given the fact that Maggie and I were doing it like monkeys, you would think that I'd have considered the possibility that my seed would find a perch in her misty jungle. For whatever reason, doing it didn't seem the same as having sex. But sex is sex! It's what people and animals do to make babies.

"Tender boobs, spotting, mood swings, peeing," I recounted.

"Maggie Corrigan is pregnant, you idiot. What the hell are we going to do?" He looked down at his nachos. "My cheese is cold! Shit!"

"Just microwave it," I said.

"I'm too overwhelmed to get up!"

So even though I was the guy with the broken butt and the potentially pregnant girlfriend, I was the one who stuck Darius's nachos back in the microwave to melt his cheese again.

Of course, I wasn't thinking about his cheese or my butt. I was thinking about Maggie.

After I delivered the heated-up nachos to Darius's lap, I moved my doughnut to the kitchen table to research early signs of pregnancy. Ms. Tindall had indeed covered all this in my freshman-year health class.

I was dumbstruck. I stared at sad Darius, who had passed out (from beer probably), his greasy nachos on his lap. I thought and thought and thought.

I thought some more.

And even some more.

Until deep into the dark night, when Darius tipped over and snored on the couch, covered in those nachos. He and his beer drinking made me sad. I pictured

Darius when he was a little boy, before beer, playing in the sandbox behind the mullet house. Mom was in her lawn chair, soaking in the sun next to him, and I pictured me as a baby bouncing on Mom's knee as she sang me hippie songs about bullfrogs and butterflies and how they get born and reborn. And then I thought about Mom covering me in her motherly kisses and Maggie covering me in different kisses, but they were still love kisses, real kisses that made my heart sing hippie songs, important kisses. And as the night got darker and deeper, I got excited because I love life. I love parents, and I love Maggie. I thought about how I wanted to make a good home for a baby because my family was all broken and sad at the moment. But I wasn't sad, and Maggie wasn't sad. Mom was gone but not sad. And you know what? I was Taco, right? I knew that I'd be a great dad, the best dad! I could pass on my mom's amazing lessons to a baby! Oh yeah, I got so, so, so warm and happy.

Maggie and I are going to have a kid! I bet she even planned for this and that's why we never discussed protection and why she wanted to have sex all the time.

Sure, I knew. The timing sucked in some ways. Teenage parenting limits your ability to…rent a limo for the prom or whatnot. Okay, there's more to it than that, but me and Maggie? We were a team, weren't we? We could be a real family. I wanted a real family. I still want a real family. I love families! And Maggie? There is nobody in the world I'd rather be up shit creek with than her. We could make lemonade out of this lemon, right?

Yes!

Family.

CHAPTER 4

I don't drive. Mom was diagnosed the day after I got my permit, and I decided I wanted to spend time with her rather than learn how. I don't bike because bike seats make my business end sore even when I'm in top condition. Due to my coccyx situation, which had by mid-October gotten a little bit better, biking was a total no go. And so on that epic Saturday morning, I set out by foot.

When I have full range of motion, it takes me about twenty-five minutes to get from my house to the Corrigans' home. But I hadn't run or really even walked any distance in seven weeks, so I made slow progress up and down the hills of Bluffton. It took me nearly an hour to get to Maggie's. Of course, if I hadn't run into Brad Schwartz and Akilesh Sharma on Main Street, it would've been more like forty minutes.

Sharma is one of my good buddies, but he'd been visiting relatives with his parents all summer and was mostly taking college classes (instead of wasting his giant Sharma brain in high school), so we hadn't spent any time together for a while. He was pretty concerned about the state of my butt. He was all, "How could such a weird injury even take place?" So to show I valued his place in my life, I took the time to explain how it happened, even though I was monkey-jacked to discuss our baby with Maggie.

No, dingus! I did not tell Sharma and Brad the good news. I'm a gentleman. I sort of believed Maggie planned for this baby. (She had to be smarter than me, right?) But I wasn't positive, and I didn't know for sure if Maggie even knew she was pregnant. Certainly I wouldn't be the one to let the mouse out of the sack with the general public.

After I left my good buds behind, I walked the last couple of autumn tree-lined blocks to the giant home inhabited by that blessed Corrigan family filled with blond girls. I figured that Mom and Dad Corrigan would be less than thrilled by the developments at hand (pregnant Maggie), so I calmed myself and thought, *Don't just blurt it out! Don't just shout it out to the whole Corrigan world!* I was excited, so it was going to be hard.

I found Mrs. Corrigan, Misha, and Molly raking leaves into a giant pile near the raised tomato bed where my butt had nearly met its death.

"Top of the morning to you, Corrigan ladies!"
I called.

All three turned to me and stared. It was the first
time I'd been to the house since the accident. I wasn't
surprised by the reception. How would you feel if you
saw the person who nearly fell to his death standing in
the very yard in which you were now playing with leaves?
I didn't blame any of them for my trouble, so I put on my
most gracious face.

"How are you all doing this fine fall day?" I asked.

Misha smiled. "Want to jump in my leaf pile, Taco?"

"It's my pile too!" Molly squealed.

"No—no jumping," Mrs. Corrigan said. "I imagine
Taco's here for Maggie."

"Right you are, Mrs. C. Maybe I can play with you
girls another time? Anyway, I'm still a little sore from
falling off your house."

"That was forever ago," Misha said.

"Maggie! Come out here!" Mrs. Corrigan hollered at
the house. "Maggie!" The whole time she shouted, she
kept her eyes on me like I might disappear if she blinked.

Finally Maggie showed up on the front porch. Even
though it was almost noon, Maggie was still wearing her
nightgown, and her hair was all twisted up into a rat's
nest, like she just pulled herself off her pillow.

"Hey there, Mags!" I waved to her.

"Hey," she said. "What do you want?"

"Can I come in? I have some big news."

"No," Mrs. Corrigan said. "You can't. I…Maggie's father is in the middle of an important project. Why don't you and Taco take a walk around the block? We'll be having lunch soon. Then we're going…we're going to Dubuque to the mall. To see a movie, so don't be long."

"We're going to Dubuque?" Molly asked.

"Yay!" Misha said.

"You have ten minutes," Mrs. Corrigan said to Maggie.

"Okay," Maggie said. She padded down the steps in her bare feet and began walking down the sidewalk, away from the house.

"Hey, wait up!" I said, but she kept walking.

"Ten minutes," Mrs. Corrigan called after us.

When I caught up to Maggie, she said, "What are you doing here? Can't you take a hint ever, Taco? You know my parents don't want you around."

"Sure. There's some bad blood, but here's what I figure: The more you know me, the more you love me. Am I right?"

Maggie looked up as she walked. She smiled a little. "That's been my experience, yeah."

43

"So maybe I should come around more so they get to know me too."

The smile slid off Maggie's perfect face. "No, that's not a good idea. I'm grounded by the way. I've actually been grounded for a while, but my parents don't know what time cheerleading practice ends, so I can come over."

"Wait. What? Why are you grounded?" I asked.

"Duh, I stayed at your house until one in the morning, and Dad had to come to get me. And he had to wait while I put on clothes."

"Aha," I said. "Why didn't you tell me?"

"I don't want to add to your burden."

"You're my girlfriend. You should be able to share your stuff with me."

"No, but—"

"And come on, my butt is healing! I'm just about fully operational at this juncture."

"Listen, I just want you to be blissfully unaware, okay?" Maggie said.

"Why?" I asked.

"Because you have a dead mom and your dad's gone and your brother drinks too much."

"Oh," I said. "Darius passed out with nachos last night."

"And your mom, Taco," Maggie said. "Your mom."

This surprised me a little bit. Nobody—and I mean nobody—ever mentioned my mom. I thought everyone had forgotten about her other than me, Dad, and my drunk brother.

"My mom and dad would've killed you by now, you know?" Maggie said. "If they didn't feel sorry for you, you'd be in jail."

Leaves were falling all around us. Orange and yellow and red. The sun was out. It was so beautiful there in Maggie's neighborhood. *Today is the best day ever.* I didn't want to dwell on the past or on who wanted to kill me or put me in jail. I wanted to talk about the future. Our future!

"Not to change the subject," I said, "but did you know you're pregnant?"

Maggie stopped cold in her tracks. She glared up at me. "What the hell, Taco?"

"I…I'm just saying," I said.

"Yeah, no shit, I know," Maggie snapped.

"Were you trying to get pregnant?" I asked.

"Jesus. No!"

That surprised me a little, dingus. "Okay. Do your parents—"

"I know, but nobody else does. I drove all the way to Dubuque for that test. How do *you* know?"

"Darius told me."

"What? Darius?"

"Yeah! I listed your symptoms because I thought you were possessed by a ghost, but he said you were pregnant. I did some independent research, which concurred with his assessment."

Maggie's face fell. "I have to do something," she said. "I'd better do something."

"Well, I was thinking," I said.

Maggie's eyes opened wide like she was totally ready for any wisdom or solution I might have to offer her. "You were?"

"Yes. And I have a plan."

Maggie exhaled hard. "Okay, good. Because I can't handle this by myself."

I grabbed her hands in my hands. "Listen. We've got this. We'll get married. You can move into the suite, and we'll raise our baby. This is great, right? Married! I want to make a family with you for sure."

Maggie yanked her hands away from me. "Shit, Taco!"

"What?"

"Just shut up! You shut up!" Maggie's head looked like it might totally explode.

"Shut up?" I asked. "Why?"

"Because! I don't want to be…I want to be on the dance team in college!" she shouted.

"That's cool. That's great," I said.

"Shit, man!" And then she took off running. I've already mentioned how amazingly fast she is, and with my unholy coccyx, there was no point in giving chase, so I just stood there and watched her tear down the street with that perfect running form that comes so naturally to her.

This probably shouldn't be a great memory. She was trying to get away from me after all. But wow. She looked so determined and powerful, you know? Plus Maggie Corrigan is killer hot. So sweet-assed hot when she starts taking off like a gazelle like that.

The memory hurts too.

I do totally love her. It hurts when you're a junkie.

CHAPTER 5

I didn't want Maggie to feel so bad. Sure, for a sixteen-year-old, getting pregnant isn't exactly living the dream when you don't want to be pregnant.

Or maybe it is, being filled with life?

Life is a gift, my mom said. Today is the best day ever, right? Today is what we've got, so what are you going to do about it? I decided I'd start learning what it was going to take to be a good dad and husband because Maggie was pregnant even if she wanted to be on a college dance team.

I brewed myself a fine hot Lipton tea, which is what my mom did when she had to concentrate on something for long hours. I sat down at the computer and began to research.

First things first. I had to figure out when our baby would enter the world.

I did some searching, some thinking. I wrote out some notes. I put a pencil behind my ear. I felt like a real adult.

I'll tell you one thing, dingus, trying to figure out a due date is no easy task. You don't just say, "Okay, September sexy plus nine months equals May, so…baby's coming in May." The pregnancy people on the Internet use some kind of higher-powered algebra to get this thing calculated. It goes something like this:

Approximate date of inception minus two weeks equals date of lady's last *little friend* plus forty weeks equals the blessed due date.

Or to put it in the mathematical shorthand, I scribbled out on my notepad:

$$DOI - 2W = DOLLLF + 40W = DD.$$

The math itself isn't so hard (other than the fact that as the guy in the relationship, I wasn't exactly sure of the lady's last little friend, so I wasn't totally sure I was getting it right). Why do I say it's higher-powered algebra then? Because check this out: From accessing my memory, I believed me and the Mags conceived our little baby right around the seventh of September, although it could've been a couple days before or a couple days after. We were doing it like monkeys around that time. I drew a monkey swinging from the vines on the calendar. Maggie was unstoppable for those few days, which I figured must be evidence that her body was craving my seed in a biological sense (ovulating), even though we were doing it for recreational purposes.

Using the seventh, I applied this formula and came up with this: Sept. 7 – 2W = Aug. 24 + 40W = May 30.

The due date! May 30 is when I would be a dad and start a new Taco family.

Then I squinted at the calculation. Something seemed nonsensical. Or maybe magical! See, according to this calculation from the expert pregnancy people on the Internet, Maggie had been pregnant since August 24. I stood up from my chair. On August 24, we were both snow-white virgins. How could she already have been pregnant? Holy, holy, holy!

The world is filled with magic. I went over to the couch, and I fell on my face because it was so crazy. Our love made Maggie pregnant when we were both still virgins. That's a miracle. That's destiny. Our child would be destiny's child.

I pictured our baby traveling to poor countries and sharing cash and vaccines and comic books with all the needy children.

I was pretty dang psyched. After I took in the immensity of it all—I did a little praying and talking to my mom via meditation—I leaped back to the computer and wrote this all in an email and sent it to Maggie.

She didn't respond right away. When she did respond, she didn't get all psyched about the miracle of the virgin pregnancy, but instead she suggested I calm down a little.

She wrote:

Yeah, that's weird, but it's only a calculation meant to figure out the due date, so I don't think there's really anything miraculous about it. Listen. Please don't be excited, Taco. I don't know what to do about anything, okay? I'm not ready to be a mom, so you know...

Well, balls! I knew what to do. Life is a miracle! Like I am and Maggie is and my mom was. It was our job to take care of it.

At school all the following week, I handed Maggie folded-up sketches I made of different master suite config-urations that would allow for a king-size bed, a crib, and a giant-screen TV. One sketch had all the junk removed, and there was straw on the floor and a manger. And I drew me and Maggie as Joseph and Mary. I drew some donkeys, camels, goats, and wise men too. She thought it was a joke, which made her laugh a little, which was nice. I missed that.

Later I redrew the master suite and added a changing table to the diagram. I also drew a sketch of the giant, wise lion (spirit animal) I wanted to paint on the suite's wall. These drawings didn't make Maggie smile. In fact, I saw her throw out my sketch of the lion like two minutes after I gave it to her. When she walked away, I ran over to the garbage and saved it. I had worked for an hour on that sucker!

For the following two weeks, Maggie barely wanted to talk. She didn't come over to visit or call the house, and even though I wanted to, I didn't go to her house. I didn't want to make her more upset.

Oh no, I didn't blame my girl. She wasn't feeling very well. I could see it in her face. Her stomach was upset. I only wished I was there in the morning to hold her hair back when she barfed.

At the end of that second week, Maggie actually missed the final football game of the season, a play-off game. We lost, which meant football cheerleading was done too. One of the other cheerleaders, Carrie Cramer, told me Maggie had the stomach flu.

I didn't say, *Oh no! Wicked morning sickness lasting all day long*, but I sure thought it.

It would've been easier if I had a cell phone so I could text. As soon as Carrie told me about Maggie, I wanted to tell Maggie how much I loved her and how it would all be okay. But I had to wait until I got home to use the computer. Then I had to wait even longer because Darius was playing *Minecraft* (even though our Internet lagged and he got killed all the time by richer fellows with computers that actually worked fast, and that shit drove him to swear and break pencils and things).

After Darius finally got too frustrated to play anymore and went to bed, I sent her a message.

Maggie, I've read up on this, and your illness will probably not last too much longer. We will be in the second trimester soon. Most ladies don't have a ton of vomiting during the second trimester. So hang tough, lady pal!

Maggie wrote back on Saturday morning.

Taco, I have been online, and supposedly the thing inside me looks like a shrimp from someone's shrimp cocktail. I'm not ready for it to turn into a baby. I have to tell my parents I'm pregnant. I think maybe I want an abortion. Probably need one. I'm sorry.

Abortion. Abortion. Abortion.
Oh no, dingus. Abortion had never occurred to me,

which is crazy because my mom was politically active about that. She was on the pro-choice team because of what she saw as a nurse. And my mom was a good person, but this didn't feel good.

I fell into my bed and cried, which I never really did before Maggie got pregnant. I didn't cry when Mom died. Not when Dad moved up north. Not when Darius got arrested. Instead of crying, I'd lie as still as a dead man in my bed, in the yard, or on the floor of the basement when it was too hot. But I never cried—not until I thought about the miracle baby being dead. I tried to lie still, but instead I wailed and soaked my sheets (just like Maggie had not too long before).

In some ways it was like all the hard things—Mom, Dad, and Darius—got wrapped up in my crying about the baby. I pictured my little miracle baby and Mom. I pictured Mom getting married to Dad. I pictured the birth of Darius and how happy Mom and Dad must've been, not knowing that he would have anger issues from a past life. I pictured Mom hugging me as a baby.

I cried so hard for so long, I threw up. Like I was the one with morning sickness. I sort of had morning sickness in a way. I was filled up with so much sadness. I felt really sad for Maggie too. She had to tell her parents that she was pregnant, which would be so tough. They had to know I was the father, a boy named Taco. So sad for everyone involved.

But today is the best day I've ever had, so…

In the afternoon I crawled out of bed and crawled to the computer and wrote:

Maggie, I support you. When you speak to your parents, please refer to me by my given name, William, and not by Taco, which is just a nickname I got because I ate so many tacos while I was in second grade.

Thank you,
William Keller

Maggie didn't write me back the rest of the day. I tried to read *The Dark Tower*, but I couldn't. I tried to do calc, but I couldn't. I tried to look at the Internet, but I couldn't. I tried to watch TV, but I couldn't. In the end, I looked at my parents' wedding album for like six hours. I stared at every single picture. Everybody was dead. Two grandparents, one mom. All their smiles, gone.

I drew a couple pictures of the baby and me kicking a soccer ball in the backyard. I couldn't make the backyard look right. It looked totally stupid. Like a little kid drew it.

I kept repeating to myself, *This is the best day ever.*

I didn't feel so great though. Not at all.

CHAPTER 6

The landline rang (well, it sort of bleats like a dying sheep) in the middle of the night. Dingus, when your mom is dead, your dad is several hundred miles away in an enormous pit mine, and your brother is Darius, calls in the middle of the night are unsettling. I jumped out of bed and ran down the hall (healing buttocks–okay running). Then I tripped on Darius, who was passed out in front of the bathroom. (This harmed my buttocks a little, but I was relieved he wasn't the source of the call.) I got to the phone in the kitchen before the thing went to voice mail.

"Are you dead, Dad?"

"Shh. It's me," said a voice.

"Shh, who?" I asked.

"Maggie," said the voice. "Can I come over? It's kind of important."

I looked at the clock on the oven, which said 8:22 p.m. I looked out the window through the back door. It was pitch-black like the devil in his dark black suit. "I think my clock is wrong. What time is it?"

"It's just after one. I don't have to come over, I guess, but I'd like to see you," Maggie whispered. "Mary will · drive me, so they won't say I stole the car."

"Who?" I asked.

"The evil, soul-crushing adults who live in my house."

"Oh."

"Can I come?"

"My door always swings on welcome hinges for you, Maggie."

"Please just cut the bullshit, Taco. I'm on my way."

In the five minutes between Maggie's shock-the-monkey call and Mary dropping her at the front door, I managed to drag Darius's unconscious body down the stairs and into his basement bedroom. Once on the way down, I kind of dropped him. He woke up super quick, smiled (upside down), pointed at me, and said, "Kayla Kronstadt is getting married."

"To who?" I asked.

"A man. But not me, because I'm a dumb-ass fish boy who wastes his life," he said. Then he sobbed or laughed and closed his eyes again.

Whatever it was that Darius poured in his mouth bled out of his pores. He was a stale stink factory. The booze smell was so big that it overwhelmed his natural fish odor. Very gross. But still, I felt terrible for him and his lost high school girlfriend. He had thought he'd marry her one day.

"I'm so sorry, Darius," I whispered. "I'm really sorry about Kayla."

Two minutes later, me with my bear claw slippers on because my feet had gotten frozen like ice cubes down in Darius's basement, I answered a quiet knocking on the door. I got there in time to see that fantastic Subaru wagon pull away from the curb.

I didn't see what shape Maggie was in until we got into the living room and I turned on the lamp. My girl looked like she'd swallowed a pail of nails. Her blue eyes were big. Her face was drained and splotchy with tears. She sat quietly on the couch and stared across the room, through the wall, out into the terrifying emptiness of space.

"You okay, Maggie?" I asked. I sat on Dad's old burgundy recliner, but I didn't recline it. I sat way forward.

"My parents didn't take the news very well."

"They're not happy about the baby?"

She turned to me. "Yeah, no shit, Taco. They're not happy, okay?"

"Okay."

Her eyes drifted back to the wall. "Mom was so pissed. I mean, she was furious. She wouldn't stop yelling. And

59

you know what? I was glad she was mad. She was right," Maggie said.

"No, she's not right," I said.

Her voice got so quiet. "She is. I'm stupid and irresponsible. Mom was so…I wish she'd killed me. I want to be dead."

"No! No, you don't!" I stood fast, crossed to the couch, and kneeled in front of her. I grabbed her hands. "No! Please don't say that stuff, Maggie. Okay?"

"Mom called me a slut," Maggie whispered. "A stupid slut. If…if anyone ever uses that word in front of her, she freaks. She says it's ignorant and violent to use that word, but she called me one anyway."

I tried to get her to look at me, but she wouldn't.

"Then I called her a hypocrite and a bitch, and Dad had to, like, bear hug her because she wanted to hit me."

"I'm sorry. I'm sorry. It'll get better. You'll feel shipshape in the morning." I wasn't sure what I was saying. That's what my mom would tell me if I got sick in the middle of the night. *You'll feel shipshape in the morning.* What the hell does that even mean? "Really. It's going to be okay, okay?"

"It's not, because I want to be dead."

"No!" I shouted. "You do not want to be dead! Because you're amazing. You're smart and good. You're radiant!"

When I said radiant, she turned from the wall and looked at me. "You're so full of shit."

"No, I'm not."

"Well, that's the thing. That's why I'm here. Dad pulled Mom away from me, and I ran upstairs. I thought I should be dead, but then I thought about you. I thought, *All that stuff Taco says about me—all that stuff he says—he believes it.*"

"Yes, I do. I'm not full of shit. I think you're the best, most beautiful person in the world," I said.

"Mary doesn't like you, but she says you really love me."

"I do. One hundred percent."

Maggie held my hands tightly. "I only feel happy when I'm with you. Even when you make me mad, I'm happy when I'm with you."

"Yeah?" I said.

"Yeah," Maggie said. "If I'm with you, then I'm okay."

"Yeah," I said.

Maggie's eyes got wet like she was about to fall asleep. "Just don't bullshit me," she whispered.

"Okay. You got it," I said.

"I need to sleep. Will you stay by me and not leave?"

"Forever, Maggie Corrigan," I said.

"Okay," she said softly. "You know when you said we should get married?"

"Yeah," I said.

"I will marry you. Let's totally get married."

I was so hopped up about all this, I couldn't sleep for like five hours. I pressed my dolphin face into Maggie's hair and pretended that we were all dolphins—me, Maggie, and our baby—and we swam and jumped super high behind a boat full of tourists in Florida. The tourists were just screaming and applauding about how high my family and I could jump. I could do dolphin backflips too.

Even though Maggie said some pretty serious and scary stuff, it seemed like we'd turned the corner. We were going to be a family for real.

Married.

I wasn't too sad about not sleeping.

CHAPTER 7

I woke up the next morning at nine thirty, the phone bleating. Usually I sleep with the curtains open, but I'd closed them when Maggie Corrigan took off her clothes during the night. Didn't want any Peeping Toms to get a glimpse. Got to protect my family! While little light penetrated the dark green fabric, I could see plenty of day seeping around the edges. The phone kept bleating.

"Ugh," I whispered. But I didn't get up, didn't go to the phone. My arms were wrapped around Maggie. We were stuck together. She didn't wake up, and I sure didn't want to wake her after how bad her night had been with her parents.

The phone stopped for a couple minutes, but then it started again.

This was enough noise to waken the zombie below. "Taco!" Darius shouted from the basement. "You up there?"

I didn't respond. A twinge of anxiety began to grow in my chest. It was slowly dawning on me that it was Monday. We weren't supposed to be sleeping. We were supposed to be at school! I began to stir, to try to gently wake up poor Maggie.

Meanwhile, Darius climbed the stairs like an angry hippo. By the time he got to the top, the phone had stopped ringing, and that made him swear. Then I heard him lift the receiver and punch in the code for the voice mail.

A few seconds later, Darius shouted from down the hall, "Hey! You here, Taco? School called to say you didn't show up to…" He stopped for a moment. Then Darius cried, "Holy shit! Is Maggie Corrigan in there? Her dad! Her dad needs to…"

"Uh-oh," Maggie said.

Darius slammed down the phone and exploded into the suite. "Dude! Did you abduct her?"

"No," Maggie said.

"Of course not," I said.

"What are you doing?" Darius cried. "I'm like your guardian, okay? I'm the one who's supposed to keep you from… I'm only twenty-one, but you have to stop this shit and listen!" His mouth hung open, and his noggin went the color of a ripe plum.

"We overslept. We're going to school now," I said.

"We are?" Maggie asked.

"We are the adults, and we are going to school. We have a quiz in English," I reminded her.

Maggie nodded. "Yeah. Right. Okay. "

"Holy shit, holy shit," Darius murmured, shaking his head.

"Please leave so Maggie and I can get prepared for the day," I said to Darius.

"Holy Christ!" he shouted. "Is that it?" His eyes looked like Ping-Pong balls. He didn't move.

"Darius, please," I said.

Then he slammed the door shut.

Without saying a word, Maggie and I pulled on our clothes. We both went into the bathroom together. She peed while I brushed my teeth, which was pretty awesome. Pretty adult, right? Then she used my toothbrush to clean her chomps.

"I look like shit," Maggie said into the mirror. "I haven't gone to school without showering since sixth grade."

"You're still a hottie," I said.

Luckily I no longer lived in the fantastic mullet house on the west side of town. That would've been a long walk, and we might've missed the quiz. The high school's only a five-minute hike from the suite. We got to school right as the bell rang between second and third period. We blended into the flow of kids in the hall, grabbed our books (and my inflatable school doughnut) from our lockers, and met in the doorway to Mrs. Mullen's junior English class. We smiled and kissed quick.

Maggie whispered, "I just realized I wasn't sick at all this morning. You can even cure morning sickness, Taco Keller."

"Yes, I can," I said. "I take care of things."

Then we started making out, blocking the door for everyone else.

"Excuse me," Mrs. Mullen said. "Could you please get your hormonal rears in your seats so I can start my class?"

Maggie Corrigan and I laughed.

Both Maggie and I aced that quiz. It was about comma use, which I totally understand. Maggie is just great at English because her dad wears those leather patches on the elbows of his English professor jacket.

Our new life together was off to such a great start. But after English, we had to split up to go to different classes. She went to gym to whack some birdies, and I went to calc, which was killer. Mr. Edwards, the calc teacher, would just split my brain in two, making us do things that were so hard and useless. That day, for instance, he stood in front of class and said, "Today we're going to construct a relatively simple model of change having to do with the speed of a cannonball."

Now I'm all about cannons. They're loud, which I

like. But I don't need an equation to know what happens to the speed of a cannonball after it's fired. I've seen it on TV. It flies through the air, slows down, and then stops eventually (usually in the hull of a ship or in the wall of an old-time army fort). Why would I need a mathematical model to predict that?

Anyway, I couldn't concentrate on cannonballs. I was worried about Maggie, worried what would happen to her, psychologically speaking, if she didn't have her old pal Taco standing by to cheer her up. If I was nearby, I could take care of things, keep her from feeling sick. But no, I had to think about cannonballs!

Mr. and Mrs. Corrigan were worried about Maggie too apparently. The school called them to let them know Maggie showed up. (School didn't call Darius to let him know I had arrived, by the way). Then the Corrigans came to school and pulled Maggie right back out of school. They took her home.

I found out in the hall after calc. Akilesh Sharma, who had passed calc as a freshman, so he wasn't in class with Brad Schwartz and me, asked, "What's wrong with Maggie Corrigan, man?"

I stopped in my tracks. "What do you mean?"

"I just saw her crying on the way to the parking lot with her parents."

"Did someone die?" Brad asked.

"Did she kill someone?" Sharma asked.

"No. Oh no!" I cried. When Maggie was with me, she felt good, healthy, happy. When she was with her parents, she wanted to die and get an abortion too.

I ran through the commons and then out into the parking lot.

But Maggie and the Corrigans were long gone.

CHAPTER 8

I fully intended to go over to the Corrigans' after school. There was no football practice to watch after we lost in the play-offs, so I had no place I needed to be. Except I had to use the bathroom.

Now I'm no prude. I'm generally game to take care of business in the public sphere if necessary. But in a fit of uncommon kindness, Darius had fitted the suite's toilet with a cushioned seat, which was necessary and soothing to my coccyx after I had sat in class all day. So instead of going directly to the Corrigans, I headed home.

At home I did my business naked because I don't like clothes getting touched by bathroom smell. And so I removed my clothes. Just before sitting down on my soft seat, however, the phone began its bleating. I sucked in a fast breath. *Maggie wants to come back!* I burst from my bathroom and ran down the hall to the kitchen. I managed to pick up the call before it went to voice mail.

"Maggie!" I shouted into the phone. There was a

pause. Then a woman said, "Might I speak to Taco if he's home. This is Taco, correct?"

"Taco's speaking because he is home," I replied. "Who is this?"

"Danielle Corrigan."

"Mrs. Corrigan!"

"Yes."

I waited for her to say something more, but she didn't. So I let fly. "Nice to hear from you," I said. "Is Maggie okay? Why'd you pull her out of school? Never mind. I'd like to talk to Maggie now."

"Of course you would," Mrs. Corrigan said. "She is your…your baby mama. Isn't that right?"

"Baby mama?" I asked. "I suppose."

"Actually, Reggie and I would both like to speak to you in person."

"Reggie and Danielle," I said.

"Right," Mrs. Corrigan said.

"And who might Reggie be?" I asked. "Mr. Corrigan?"

"Of course, Taco," said Mrs. Corrigan. "Would you please come over?"

Well, dingus, I was aching from the day and still hadn't grabbed my me time on the foam-padded throne. Maybe it was weird to ask, but I asked, "I'm a little busy, and my health still isn't what it should be. Would you mind sending a car for me?"

"You don't mind sneaking over here in the middle of the night, but you'd like a ride when we invite you?"

"It's been a tough day, Danielle," I said. "I'm hurting. Coccyx, you understand."

There was a pause on the other end, during which Darius entered the house carrying a couple Dairy Queen Blizzards. His mouth dropped open when he saw me standing naked while talking on the telephone.

"I'll have Mary come get you," Mrs. Corrigan finally said.

"Thank you. Give me a few minutes," I replied.

Mrs. Corrigan hung up.

Darius stared at my unsheathed body. "Things are outer limits, man. Totally, totally outer limits," he said.

I hung up the receiver and hobbled back to the throne room.

Darius chased after me with the Blizzards. "We have to talk. I bought you a Blizzard, so you'll talk."

"I can't talk to you right now, okay?" I said. "I have to go to the Corrigans' to talk about this situation with them."

"They know?" Darius asked.

"Yes," I said.

"Thank God, man," Darius said. "They're adults.

They can figure this shit out." He paused for a moment. "I'm going to eat both Blizzards, you jerk."

I wanted that Blizzard, but Darius's face was all red from the stress of this situation. "Okay," I said. "Thanks for getting it for me, and you should have both. You deserve both."

"Shut up," Darius said.

"Don't worry, Darius. This is a great day…just like every day."

"Seriously. Shut up."

Twenty minutes later I was in the Corrigans' fantastic Subaru with Mary. "How are you?" I asked.

"I'm fine. Thanks," she replied.

Mary is two years older than Maggie. Mary is spending one year taking care of her general ed credits in town at the college before she goes to Scotland to study medieval history for the next three years. Amazing, right? Mary is a hottie, but she's also a total dweeb who sings Shakespeare songs at the Renaissance fest. Something about her nerdliness makes me feel very comfortable around her (even when she's mad at me). If she has the courage to go out in public dressed like an elf princess and sing songs at the top of her lungs, she must be pretty strong and courageous in her heart, right? That's what I think. I like that Mary Corrigan a hell of a lot. I sort of think of her as my older sister.

"College going well?" I asked her.

"Would you please not say another word to me? You cause too much trouble."

I nodded. "You got it," I said. Sort of hurt my feelings, but I understood.

When we pulled up to the Corrigan home, Maggie was sitting out front with her head in her hands.

"Look what you've done to her," Mary said.

"She's not sad when she's with me," I replied. "Maybe you did it to her."

We climbed out of the car and walked toward the house. You think I was nervous about this meeting, dingus? Talking to the parents of the girl who got knocked up through our love? No way. Not even remotely. I looked forward to it.

When I got to the porch, Maggie stood and hugged me hard. I smiled at her. She said, "Thanks for coming over. It takes a lot of guts."

I squeezed her hands. "It just takes love."

"Barf," said Mary. "I'm going to my room."

The Corrigans, both Danielle and Reggie, were seated at the big dining room table. They cupped mugs of steaming tea in their hands. They both slouched. They looked a little rough around the edges.

Missy, who's an eighth grader, was in the room

adjacent to the dining room, plunking out some classical tune on the piano. Misha and Molly, the young ones, made glitter art on newspapers that were spread across the floor.

"Would you three please either go outside or up to your rooms?" Mrs. Corrigan asked.

The three youngest Corrigans immediately stood and left. What great kids, huh?

Maggie and I sat next to each other at the table.

"Would you like something to drink, Taco?" Mr. Corrigan asked.

"Yes, thanks," I replied. "Do you have any Liptons?"

"No," Mrs. Corrigan said. "It's time to talk. Like adults. This is an adult situation."

"If this is an adult situation, Taco should be able to have some tea," Maggie said.

"Taco. Taco. Taco," Mrs. Corrigan snapped.

"Danielle is very upset," Mr. Corrigan said to me.

"And you're not?" Mrs. Corrigan asked Mr. Corrigan.

"I don't need any tea," I said. I didn't want to upset Mrs. Corrigan any more than necessary. "I'm good."

"Wrong," Mrs. Corrigan said. "Not good. My daughter is pregnant."

"It's true," I said. "Our intent was pure, however. I love your daughter."

Mr. Corrigan smiled for a moment. Mrs. Corrigan clenched her jaw.

"I love Taco too," Maggie said.

"So what are we going to do about it?" Mrs. Corrigan asked me. "Maggie tells me an abortion is off the table. Do you agree, Taco?" Mrs. Corrigan once again spat my name, which was not my given name.

"Call me William. And I agree. This is our baby," I said. "It may be a miracle baby."

"Oh God," Mr. Corrigan said and sighed.

"You're sixteen," Mrs. Corrigan said sternly. "You're a baby."

"Seventeen in a month," I offered.

"You don't drive," Mrs. Corrigan said.

"Not interested in driving," I said.

"You don't have a job," Mrs. Corrigan said.

"Up to this point, I've been too involved in school activities to find time for gainful employment. But my family comes first. I'll begin a job search pronto."

"Oh my God. Oh my God." She closed her eyes and put her head in her hands. "We're going to end up raising this baby, Reggie," she said.

That set a fire under the professor's rear. "We should discuss adoption," he said.

"No!" Maggie shouted. "This is my baby! You can't give away my baby!"

"I'm not giving away your baby—just suggesting that you'd be doing a wonderful thing for a couple and for *your* child if you did. You'd be giving the gift of your love to people who—"

"No!" Maggie cried. Tears began sliding from her eyes. That set a fire under me.

"I hear you, sir. Love is a wondrous gift. Very wonderful. But first and foremost, my job is to support the emotional needs of my wife."

"Your wife?" Mr. Corrigan repeated.

"You didn't. You couldn't," Mrs. Corrigan said to Maggie.

"They couldn't," Mr. Corrigan said. "They're minors."

"We could if we had your permission," I said.

Mrs. Corrigan stood up. She held her teacup so tightly, it looked as if she would crush it. Then she whipped that teacup onto the wood floor so it smashed into a million pieces.

We all jumped.

"Jesus, mom! Psycho much? You think I'm crazy? I learned from the best!" Maggie cried.

Mrs. Corrigan glared at Maggie. "Shut your mouth." She turned and took off into the kitchen, cursing us all out under her breath. Maggie kicked back her chair, cursed, and chased after her mom like she was a dog going after a stick somebody threw.

A moment later, shouting came from the kitchen.

Meanwhile, Mr. Corrigan and I sat in the dining room. I smiled at him. Mom had told me to smile if I was ever confused because I have a nice smile. I didn't know what else to do. Our meeting wasn't going very well.

Mr. Corrigan shook his head. "Taco," he said. "This is real. This is happening."

"I get it," I said. "Reality."

"Danielle has been in counseling to deal with anger. Maggie too. This situation…this fighting?" Mr. Corrigan pointed at the kitchen door and shook his head. He looked so sad. "These are two people I love who are liable to destroy each other. Can you help me please?"

I took a deep breath. I wasn't really sure what he was asking. But I wanted to help him, and I figured if I helped Maggie, I was also helping him. "I will do everything I can," I said.

Mr. Corrigan nodded. "I'll help you if you help me."

In the kitchen Maggie screamed stuff I won't repeat. Mrs. Corrigan screamed back. Some glasses broke.

"I think you should leave now. We'll talk again soon," Mr. Corrigan said.

"I'm worried about Maggie. Danielle…Mrs. Corrigan won't accidentally stab her or make her want to die or anything?" I asked.

"No, Danielle loves Maggie very much," Mr. Corrigan said. "This is just a hard time."

Because Maggie seemed so sad when she came to my house the night before and because it was her mom who caused her to be so sad, I didn't know if I should believe Mr. Corrigan, you know? My mom would never have made me feel like that. My mom also told me to be polite and respectful though, and Mr. Corrigan was a good and trustworthy person who would protect his daughter, so I decided to believe him. I took a deep breath and said, "Please tell Maggie to contact me at her earliest convenience."

Mr. Corrigan looked a bit startled. "Will do," he said.

I stood up. "Should I ask Mary for a ride?"

A large plate or maybe a platter crashed in the kitchen.

Mr. Corrigan shut his eyes. "No, you walk, Taco. Think about what's happening and what we discussed."

I nodded at Mr. Corrigan. "Okay. That sounds good." I reached out my hand so we could shake on it.

Mr. Corrigan stared at my hand for a moment. He smiled really sad, but he didn't take it.

From the kitchen Mrs. Corrigan screamed, "His name is Taco! Taco! Taco!"

"It's William," Maggie hollered.

"Better run along, son," Mr. Corrigan said.

I smiled, but it wasn't my best smile because I felt pretty sick to my stomach from all this. Then out the door I went.

On the walk home, I wondered what Mr. Corrigan was getting at with his comment about Mrs. Corrigan and Maggie's counseling. Anger? Is that why people go to counseling? I thought, *Maybe Darius should go to counseling*. That seemed so dumb though, because Darius wasn't crazy. He just drank too much and was born mad.

Then I thought about Mrs. Corrigan breaking that glass. I thought, *What you saw was real, Taco. It really happened.*

No duh, dingus.

On I walked, and I worried. What if Maggie's parents really thought she was crazy, not just mad? What if they took Maggie away and stuck her in an insane asylum or something?

I thought, *Mr. Corrigan can help me if I help him? What does that even mean?*

Then right by this giant lawn next to the old Roundtree Building, the first building ever built for the college, I saw some barn swallows chasing each other like *Star Wars* swamp speeders. Those damn birds can fly, pal!

Zigzag! Zigzag!

Super cool.

Birds don't worry.

CHAPTER 9

The Corrigans didn't send Maggie away to an insane asylum. They sent her to the suite. Seriously!

Mr. Corrigan himself called around 9:00 p.m. that night. I lumbered down the hall. (I needed a good night's rest to recover after all that walking.) Then I grabbed the bleating phone.

"I'd like to drop off Maggie, Taco," Mr. Corrigan said.

"Tonight?"

"Now," Mr. Corrigan said. "We're at our wits' end over here. She and her mother need space, and I don't know what else to do. So…now?"

"That's a surprise, Reggie, but you got it. Bring her over," I said. "I can be the responsible party."

He cleared his throat. "Maggie says your father knows about the pregnancy and supports her staying with you while we sort all this out. Is that true?"

I bit my lip on that one. I figured Dad wouldn't be very supportive, but that wasn't really the point at the moment. Maggie clearly needed to get out of the house or Reggie wouldn't be yammering on the horn at me, so I bluffed, which I'm not proud of. "My father believes Maggie and I should be together, yes."

"Uh-huh," Mr. Corrigan said. "Is there a number where he can be reached?"

"No. He's on the open road. Trucking," I explained.

"And he doesn't carry a cell phone?" Mr. Corrigan asked.

"No, sir. He thinks cell phones cause blindness and brain cancer." This wasn't true, but my mom believed that, so it seemed plausible.

"Fine. When you next speak with him, please ask him to call me to discuss our situation. In the meantime, I'd like to drop off Maggie," Mr. Corrigan said.

"Sweet ass," I said after I hung up.

Ten minutes later Maggie knocked on the front door. She was carrying an overnight bag. I let her in without a word. Mr. Corrigan waited in front of the house to see that she got in safely. I gave him a smile and a big wave. He nodded and then eased the car away from the curb and disappeared into the Bluffton night.

Was this helpful? Was I helping? Mr. Corrigan wanted help. This is the kind of thing he was talking about, right? I help Maggie, and I help him at the same time.

Maggie went directly back to my room. There, she removed her jacket, her shirt, her pants, her bra, and her panties. I watched all this action from just inside the door because I wanted her to have privacy if Darius came upstairs. She turned around slowly to face me. The blood was pumping all over my monkey body at that point, of course.

Everything changes so damn fast that you're lucky your head doesn't get twisted right off from all the spinning. Six months earlier I hadn't ever kissed a girl, much less had a naked one in my suite—a naked one who was pregnant with my miracle baby. And therein lay the rub. The babe.

"Make love to me, Taco," Maggie said.

Well, that hadn't been on the table since I found out about the baby, you know? "Uh. Is that a legit move?"

"Legit? What do you mean? Like legal?"

"Well, I don't mean legal. I mean, the cops never occurred to me, but we should google that too. Is it legal to have sex when you're pregnant in Wisconsin?"

"Jesus. I'm sure it is," Maggie said. She paused. "I'm pretty sure."

"Awesome," I said. "But we don't want to traumatize the baby with our bumping."

"The baby is like the size of a strawberry," Maggie said.

"With tiny little hands," I said. "I've done the research."

"The baby won't know about why it's bumping, and I need you."

"You do?"

"Yes."

"Oh," I said.

And so, pal, it happened. But holy balloons, I did not enjoy it, which again is something I could never have imagined even a few days earlier.

Afterward, Maggie cried and cried. I held her in my arms and comforted her, and she made the suite sheets soggy. Turns out Maggie's mom had said some pretty horrible things to her that I can't even repeat. Maggie's mom had slapped her too.

I would never slap the person I love. I'd keep her safe forever and ever. I'd fight off any invaders with every ounce of my strength for her! That's how it should be, right?

My mom would never have slapped me either. This is what I don't understand: Can a mom even call herself a mom if she's slapping her own pregnant daughter? My mom loved me and Darius no matter what, even when we made it hard.

And we did.

Take Darius. He never did well in school, and he

used to have what Dad called *a smart mouth*, meaning he'd back-talk and say crappy things to Mom and Dad when they got on his case about school or whatnot. Dad would sometimes shout or growl at Darius—but not my mom. My mom would say, "I'm sorry you're struggling, sweet boy. I'm sorry you're at odds with the world. Go down to your room and be quiet. I promise if you stop fighting, the situation will get better."

Darius might shout, "I don't fight! Mrs. Wilson (or Faherty or Treine or Mr. Bachman) is just stupid!"

But Mom would say, "Shh, sweet boy. Shhhh. Go be quiet now."

And she was right. By dinnertime, Darius was always calmer. Then she and Darius would talk about what happened and make a plan to make everything better. Mom was great at that. I sort of wish my mom was Maggie's mom because Maggie could use a little quiet time and care, but then maybe Maggie wouldn't be who she is. Also Maggie would be my sister, which would be pretty weird. And probably illegal.

Anyway, slapping the person you love is wrong.

Before I went to sleep, I set an alarm. (Maggie had already passed out.) I usually don't need one, given how my excitement for the coming day wakes me up. But after our tardiness that morning, I also set the clock on the stove.

Darius got home from his night shift at Captain Stabby's while I was in the kitchen.

"That clock has never been right," he said. "Not since we moved in."

"Yeah, man," I said. "I just noticed! I reset the time before I set the timer."

"It's bothered me for like a year," he said.

"Really? Why didn't you fix the bugger?" I asked.

He stared at me for a moment as if I had two heads. "I take care of you, not me," he said and went downstairs.

"Oh," I said to the place where Darius had been standing.

I stumbled down the hall into the suite, fell into bed, and fell asleep. Like totally fell, dingus. Like off a cliff. Morning came like hitting the damn canyon floor.

Maggie went out of her mind when the stove buzzer fired up in the kitchen.

She shot out of bed. "What time is it?"

"Seven, baby doll," I whispered. "We got a full hour and ten to get to first period."

"Jesus, Taco! Why didn't you wake me up? I can't go to school like a dirt ball again. I have to shower and blow-dry my hair. I hate it when my hair's wet. Everybody looks at you like you're a skeez if your hair's wet!"

"A what?" I asked, still groggy.

Maggie ran into the suite's throne room. "Where the hell's the shower? Didn't I see a shower in here before?" she screamed. "You don't have a shower?"

"It's in the bathroom in the hall. You might want to turn it down a couple decibels because Darius worked late and he can't find the sandman too easy after slinging fish for eight straight. Know what I mean?"

Maggie charged past me into the hall. I slid out of bed and followed. She stood in the middle of the bathroom, staring down at the toilet and the bathtub. She acted appalled.

And I was a little pissed! As if having a private throne room inside your own bedroom isn't fancy enough. Like there should by definition be a shower in every bathroom. As if the shared shower in the hall (only shared with Darius!) was like having to take a shower at the damn zoo.

"Do you even have clean towels?" Maggie cried.

"Whoa, lady. Hold on. I do laundry twice a week," I said. "Of course there are clean towels." I pride myself on my fresh spring breeze fragrance, pal.

"Well, show me how the shower works. Show me where the soap is. Give me a clean towel. I don't have any time!"

Man, did my sweet Maggie blow her top when she

found out I don't own a hair dryer. "I would've brought Mary's if I thought you didn't have one!" She was *en fuego*! (I learned that in Spanish class.)

We did finally get to school though. I did some birdie-whacking in gym to work out my anguish. And by English, Maggie had chilled out too. I guess her hair was finally dry, which helped. In the doorway to the classroom, she kissed me and whispered, "Thanks for taking care of me."

Yes! That's Taco, taking care of business.

In English, I couldn't concentrate, so I started writing lists. When Mom was super sick, she made lists that she'd give Darius (and sometimes me). She told us that writing out her responsibilities and then fulfilling her responsibilities was how she acted like an adult, how she took care of her kids and her business, and because she couldn't be the adult because of her pain and exhaustion and lack of ability to breathe, we had to do it for her (mostly Darius). So I wrote out a list because I wanted to be an adult, wanted to take care of my wife. (Well, really girlfriend, but weren't we acting married with her living in my house?)

1. Buy hair dryer.

2. Wake Maggie early as hell.

3. Install shower in suite. (Build an addition to house?)

4. Get job to earn money to buy hair dryer, alarm clock, and build addition to house.

I felt pretty good. Like I knew what I was up against and I had a plan to get the job done. When the bell rang, Maggie kissed me hard.

I was so caught up in my adult thoughts that I walked smack into Mr. Lecroy, the choir director, while I was switching classes.

"Taco. Taco Keller!"

I'm a big fan of choir. I'm not the best singer, but I love it! Anyway, I've always liked to perform, always played super minor parts in plays and musicals. (My mom loved going to the high school musical every year.) And I've always really liked Mr. Lecroy. "Hey, hey, Mr. L.," I said back.

"I didn't see your name on the musical chorus audition sign-up," he said. "I assume you ran out of time yesterday."

Whoa. With so much going on, I completely forgot about the musical. "I guess I forgot," I said.

"No," he said. "Don't forget."

I thought about Maggie and the baby and our lack of a hair dryer over at the suite. "I'm crazy busy right now," I said.

"Not too busy, I hope."

"Maybe?" I said.

"Fine. You need enticement? Keep it under your hat." Mr. Lecroy looked around at the flow of students passing us by and then leaned in to whisper. "We're doing *Wizard of Oz*!"

"Rock on," I said. "Those flying monkeys scare the shit out of me!"

"Me too!" Mr. Lecroy said. "And guess what?"

"What?"

"I have my eye on you."

"You do?" I asked.

"Mayor of Munchkinland?"

"Oh yeah?" Oh, that hurt. Mayor of Munchkinland is a kick-ass part.

"But you have to play to win, my friend. I'll be scheduling auditions the week after Thanksgiving. I won't be putting together a dream team from kids who aren't ready to make the commitment. Do you understand?"

"Yes. Understood, Captain," I said. *Crap*, I thought.

Mr. Lecroy winked, smiled. "Good."

I sprinted off to my next class but stopped after

about ten steps. I had to bend over and catch my breath. For a moment I thought I might lose my beans right there in the Bluffton High hallway. The musical is one of my favorite times of the year. It's all snowy and elfin and magical. And my friends and I all sing for hours and hours every day. Oh no, I didn't want to miss out, dingus. But…

Maggie Corrigan is having our baby, and I need to buy her a hair dryer, I thought.

Then the bell rang, and I had to get to class.

Calc was a total disaster. First, I was late, which made Mr. Edwards grimace. Second, I'd left my butt pillow in English. Third, Mr. Edwards gave a pop quiz.

Even though I'd struggled to understand calc, I'd never bombed the shiz. In fact, all through high school, I always did pretty well on tests. But I only got, like, halfway done by the time Mr. Edwards picked up my paper. Felt like I got kicked in the salad by a wild donkey. At the same time, my unwell backside throbbed from its bone-to-plastic situation without a doughnut.

I felt really defeated and in need of love. And Mr. Lecroy was all in my business again during choir that afternoon, so I couldn't help it. After choir, I slid out into the hall like a ninja and put my name on the audition sheet for *The Wizard of Oz*, even though I knew in my guts I should be thinking about cash flow and diaper budgets, not being Mayor of Munchkinland.

Oh, I didn't feel good about myself, dingus.

Maggie and I met up right after the last bell. She looked at me, concerned. "Are you tired? Do I make you tired?"

"No way," I said. "You're the sunshine." But clearly I didn't act like she was the sunshine because I could barely pick up my feet. I was so damn tired.

"Hey, now," she said. "We need to put a little pep in your cucumber!"

That made me smile. We walked home, hand in hand, making jokes the whole way. And yeah, dingus, she was sunshine because my energy really did grow back like a dandelion in the sun!

At the suite we picked up the money I had stowed in the grocery kitty and walked over to the Piggly Wiggly, still making jokes and kissing every block or two. At the Pig, we bought her a very cheap hair dryer and a frozen pizza for our dinner. Back home we watched TV in the living room and ate pizza and held hands like a happy old married couple.

At one point Maggie, whose head was resting on my shoulder, looked up at me and said, "Would you ever want to live by the ocean, Taco?"

"Of course I would. If you're there, the ocean is as beautiful as Wisconsin."

"I like whales," she whispered. "I could be a marine biologist."

"Then I'll clean the beach sand off our patio, and I'll cook you pizzas for when you get home," I said.

"I really love you, Taco," Maggie said.

I loved that evening. All in all, even with the musical trouble and failing my calc quiz, it was the best day I ever had.

CHAPTER 10

Maggie stayed at the master suite until Thursday night.

On Wednesday after school, Mr. Corrigan came over with Misha and Molly and brought us a chicken dinner. That was good because I could've scrounged up some spaghetti and butter or something, but it wouldn't have been top-notch, which is what Maggie expected in life. She'd been living with two parents who had money. I actually spent part of the afternoon having little anxiety attacks about what would happen when Maggie figured out we were essentially foodless at the house (not by my standards but by hers). Would she throw a big hissy fit and indict my character? I will never know because Mr. Corrigan and chicken came to the rescue!

We ate at our dining room table. (I had to move Mom's desktop computer, which blocked a third of the surface, and Darius was none too pleased when he got home and wanted to play *Minecraft*, which made me scared to ask him for some extra food money.) Misha and Molly stared at us while we ate as if Mags and I were wild creatures from space. They mostly stared at Maggie.

Actually, I had to stare a little bit too. Maggie was jamming that chicken into her mouth like she'd just gotten out of jail or something, like that chicken was the best thing she'd ever chomped down.

"You eat like Cookie Monster," Misha said.

Molly laughed.

"Shut up," Maggie said.

"Maggie," Mr. Corrigan said. "Be kind."

"Sorry," Maggie said.

Then Mr. Corrigan said, "Have you been getting enough to eat, honey?"

Maggie looked at me for a blink and then said, "I think so. Taco's been really good about filling my plate, Dad. We had pizza last night and toast for breakfast."

"Okay," Mr. Corrigan said. "But you need protein."

Of course, protein! She needed protein. And of course, I wanted to fill the plate of my pregnant girl. I wanted to mash her all the potatoes she could eat, grind her sausages, stir her cheese in a thousand stainless steel vats, but—money. How could I procure foodly riches for my queen without money? Well, I couldn't. Duh.

On Thursday after school, I'd hoped we'd find Darius

at home. He always gave me money when we were running low on food. He acted pissed about it sometimes because we didn't have much cash, but he still gave me some. But he wasn't around, and the cupboards were bare—other than spaghetti.

I tried to think. My personal piggy bank had dried up as soon as my allowance disappeared, which was when Mom died. I actually had a bank account with all my swimming pool money, but Darius took the ATM card and hid the passbook. He said that money was meant for me to go to college, not to use on burritos or whatever. I didn't know what to do. I had no access to capital, and Darius was at work. We could've gone to Captain Stabby's, I guess. But Maggie hated fish, and that place smelled like a bunch of dead fish.

Maggie sighed. She was super tired and slow. She sighed again.

I said, "I'm sorry."

Then she got on the horn to her dad. She whispered. She nodded. She hung up. "Let's go over to my place," Maggie said.

I really didn't want to, but I agreed. I wanted to help Mr. Corrigan help Maggie (because I would be helping Maggie by doing so).

Mary showed up about ten minutes later. With

trepidation, I got in the fantastic Subaru's backseat and rode across town to the Corrigans'.

Hearty protein-rich meat lasagna with a big salad on the side, bread sticks, iced tea, and flourless brownies for desert—this was the proper grub for my pregnant lady. And I couldn't provide it. I felt very lacking.

Other than Mrs. Corrigan, no one spoke to me during dinner. Not the little girls, not the big girls, not Mr. Corrigan, not even Maggie herself. Only Mrs. Corrigan said anything. As I sat down at the table, she asked me if I knew anything about Balinese chicken curses, and then she glared at me for the rest of the meal.

Curses?

The other Corrigans chatted over and around me. They spoke of music lessons and dance lessons and hikes they might go on the following summer and Thanksgiving in Ohio. They were spending the whole following week with their grandma near Cleveland. I'd assumed Maggie wouldn't go and would be with me, which wasn't very bright on my count. I tried to say something, but my voice disappeared like no one could hear me, no one other than Mrs. Corrigan, who gave me that Balinese chicken curse stink eye.

After dinner Maggie decided to stay in her own house because she needed protein for breakfast. She walked me out onto the porch. "Listen, Taco, I make some money at Dairy Queen, but we'll need a ton more if we're going to do this on our own. I have to eat so much right now. It's crazy how many calories I can suck down."

"I know," I said. "You're like a she-tiger."

"Go get a really good job. Then we can get married and start our family, okay? I know that seems hard, but, like, it's all you have to do, so maybe it's not that big a deal," she said.

"Yeah." I repeated, "Not that big a challenge."

Getting a really good job was actually pretty complicated—and not just because I'd signed up for musical auditions. Mom wanted me to be a kid and to concentrate on school. She didn't want me working. Even though Darius isn't the best stand-in parent, he really grabbed hold of that no-work deal, and he followed through on his promises. Still, I had to do it. I had to get a job. I couldn't be a kid anymore. A dad (like me) had to do what a dad had to do.

Maggie said she had to go to bed because she was tired. I kissed her. She smiled. She went back in the house, and I put my face against the window and watched her climb the stairs to her room.

On my walk across town, it was super dark and sad.

When I finally made it home, I found Darius passed

out on the front steps. I dragged him inside, and he promptly threw up on the living room carpet. I got him some water. He said, "Kayla won't stop breaking up with me, and now she's getting married. And you…you… you. I want to die, dude."

"Holy balls," I said. "This isn't good."

"It's not good!" Darius cried.

Poor Darius needed my help. I got him ibuprofen from the medicine cabinet. He really needed me to be an adult too, right?

That night I dreamed about a wooden chicken statue that came to life. And I knew we were in terrible trouble, dingus.

CHAPTER 11

Maggie didn't show up at school on Friday. I looked for her in the commons, where she often sat yacking with her fellow cheer girls. She wasn't there. Later I eagerly awaited her arrival in English. No go. I began to panic. After English, instead of going to calc like I should've, I went to the computer lab to check my email. She'd written me a note.

> Hey, man, I'm so tired right now. Mom and Dad are taking me to the doctor. It's just a regular check-up. Don't worry. I'll call you later.

The thought of Maggie in a paper hospital gown, all alone, her bare butt hanging loose for all to see, getting diagnosed without me, her husband who is not yet her husband, nearly caused me to run over to Southwest Municipal Hospital Clinics so that I could be by her side.

But, no…no. My mom used to tell Darius not to go off "half-cocked." I had no idea what that meant, but my mom knew everything. And I'd had that dream the night before about the chicken statue, right?

Chicken statue.

During the hearty lasagna dinner at the dinner table in the Corrigans' home, Mrs. Corrigan's constant stink eye scared me. She was a scary person not just for regular reasons. Here's the truth: Mrs. Corrigan actually had access to curses, wooden chickens, and magical knowledge from the nation of Bali.

Maggie told me about it earlier in the summer because I had picked up and played with this wooden chicken statue thing that was on a side table at Maggie's house. "Put that down!" Maggie said. "Never touch that chicken!"

"What?" I said. "Why?"

"When she was in college, Mom ran away with her crazy anthropology professor. She followed him to Bali, and she learned all about witchcraft and casting curses on people she hates."

"So?" I said. "She doesn't hate me, right?"

"That chicken is part of the witchcraft," Maggie said.

I put the chicken back down very carefully.

"Your mom ran away with her professor?" I asked. "How old was he?"

"Sh," Maggie had said. "Don't ever mention that again."

But I was very interested in the story, so I had asked Maggie more about it later. Mrs. Corrigan wasn't married yet. At the time, she was just some young girl named Danielle. Her professor was fifty-two! Danielle's own mother had to go to Bali and pay the police to basically kidnap her back. It took Mrs. Corrigan a whole year to get her head on straight and go to another college. That was where she met young Reggie Corrigan and got pregnant with Mary.

Point is that Mrs. Corrigan knew Balinese witchcraft, dingus. Put that together with my bad dream about the wooden chicken statue and my own sweet mom's warning to Darius about going off "half-cocked," and I lost my nerve. I worried that if I tried to intervene and go to the clinic, maybe I'd wake up with my eyes pecked out by a Balinese chicken (which was part of the dream I had the night before). Terrifying!

In retrospect, I believe I was overthinking. This overthinking caused a larger crisis. Going off half-cocked can cause lots of trouble too. What's the right way to be? Life can be perplexing.

Anyway, instead of running out of the building, I ran to calc. I was late, and Mr. Edwards was handing back our quizzes from earlier in the week. He looked at me, shook his head, and pointed at my grade. I got a fat effenheimer on it.

"I always thought you were a math guy, Taco" Mr. Edwards said. "You might not have the chops for calculus though."

Never before had I gotten an effenheimer on anything. Yet there it was, red and gory, scrawled across the top of the page. I choked up.

A few minutes later, Mr. Edwards gave us a problem to work on and left the classroom.

Brad Schwartz leaned over to me. "You're coming undone, dude," he whispered.

"Truth," I said.

"Sharma and I'll tutor you this weekend," Brad said. "We'll get your wheels back on track."

"Only if Maggie doesn't need me," I said.

"Man, Taco. What's up with you two?" Brad asked. "Something's afoot. Something bad. Am I right?"

"No. It's all good," I whispered, still choked up.

"Yeah, but that F isn't going away, Taco. You'll see it again and again if you don't catch up. This weekend, okay? Seriously, I'll help you," Brad said.

What good would I be to my baby and to Maggie if I flunked calc? I'd be like Darius, unable to move forward in life, stuck in the past, making deep-fried fish forever. I looked at Brad. "Affirmative," I said. "Thanks, brother. Thanks for being a great friend."

"You got it," Brad said.

I had to do better, be better, dingus.

After school I went straight home, even though a bunch of the choir peeps were meeting to practice songs from *The Wizard of Oz*. If you've never stood around a piano with a bunch of bird-singing ladies and sweet-voiced dudes to learn new music, you haven't lived, pal. It's always hilarious and like a party, and at the same time, you learn the shiz, so it's both entertaining and enlightening.

But I had no time for that because I had to be better, and that meant taking care of Maggie, being ready for her phone call. I didn't know how long her doctor appointment would take, so she could call at any moment. She might have already left a message on the suite answering machine. I ran home as best I could and burst in the door to check for messages, but she hadn't called yet, so I boiled some water for some buttered spaghetti and pulled a dining room chair into the kitchen. I sat by the phone and waited and waited and ate spaghetti and waited.

I sat from twilight to total darkness, staring at the phone that did not bleat. I stood up, sat down, walked in circles, boiled more spaghetti, and sat down, and paranoia started to choke me very badly. Paranoia made me twitch and twist from the inside out. *Is it because you're a poor Taco? A jobless Taco? Did she stop loving you? No!*

Maggie Corrigan didn't call. I didn't want to interrupt her at her doctor's appointment, but by 7:45, I figured the clinic had to be long closed.

Wait till eight. Be reasonable, I told myself.

At 8:00 p.m., I called her cell. It went straight to voice mail.

At 8:05 p.m., I looked in the *Bluffton Journal* job ads online and found an ad for a dance instructor at I Could Dance All Night, a studio downtown where I've seen little girls dressed in puffy ballerina costumes. I called over to I Could Dance All Night. A woman answered. Loud music echoed in the background.

I spoke loudly so she could hear me. "I'd like to be a dance instructor. I'm a good dancer."

The woman shouted, "Great! Where did you train?"

"I'm freestyle. I dance in my bedroom and at prom."

"Oh," the woman shouted. "Sorry! I need a certified instructor. It's in the ad."

I looked at the computer and saw she spoke the truth. "Shit."

"Bye now," the dance lady said.

At 8:25 p.m., I called the Corrigans' landline, a phone that sat on a table next to—wait for it—the same decorative, multicolored, wooden chicken statue from Bali that I'd picked up early in the summer and dreamed about the night before. My mind was really going. No one answered.

Hi. Taco Keller here. Just wondering about... Just calling to get an update on the situation over there. Maggie and the baby. Give me a quick honk on the horn if you have a chance. Thanks so much. This is Taco, by the way. I think I mentioned that...

I waited until 9:00 p.m. Then I pulled on my coat and hoofed it over to the Corrigans'. My ass hurt something special, but I couldn't be stopped.

The Corrigan house was pitch-dark. No light, no life. I rang the bell.

Nothing.

I yelled for Maggie from the sidewalk.

Nothing.

I eyeballed the side of the house and took a deep breath. Then up I went. My plan was to go in through Maggie's bedroom window, take a peak around, and gather some clues as to the Corrigans' whereabouts. But halfway up, my coccyx screaming from exertion, the floodlights flashed on and the alarm began screaming. I nearly fell off the house again, dingus. I froze for a few moments. Afraid to go up or down. What if I fell on my tender ass again? Death?

Then I came to my senses. With the alarm firing like that, cops were likely on the way!

I climbed down slow, careful. When I got to the first-floor window, there, where it hadn't been lit before, I could see a lamp sitting on the table next to the phone, sitting on the table next to the ornate Balinese chicken statue from my dream! The chicken was staring at me, pal! Seriously!

I didn't fall, but I almost did. Instead I clung to the vines as the alarm blared and the neighbors came out. Soon the cops came too.

"What in Sam Hill are you doing, Taco?" Officer Mike Peders asked after he'd pulled me to the ground.

"I don't know. I don't know," I said.

"What am I supposed to do?" Mike Peders asked the other cop. I didn't know him. "I don't want to arrest the poor kid."

"Well, hell. All these neighbors are out here watching. We can't just give him a talking to and let him walk. He can't climb people's houses. Folks are going to look for news about this in the paper," the other officer said. "Maybe trespassing?"

"Dave, come on. That's a class A. He gets Judge Hammond, and he might find himself in the clink for thirty days."

"No, please," I said. "I'm not trespassing. This is my girlfriend's house."

"Yeah, no shit, Taco. That alarm is supposed to keep the place Taco-proof," Mike said. "Maybe it's got to be trespassing?"

Well, I got real lucky right then, dingus. Another police car pulled up, and it was Mr. Frederick. He and I go way back. His son, Cody, was the assistant coach for my little league team when I was a kid. Cody loves me. He's in college up at La Crosse—second-team quarterback up there. Ever since Mom died, Cody emails me every month or so. His dad is really smart too. Mr. Frederick is a sergeant or something. Not just a regular cop.

He got out of his car and shook his head. "Damn it, Taco," he said to me.

"Sorry, sir," I said.

"This is real, you know?"

"Real?" I said. "I know."

"Mike, just bring him in. Janice will set the charge later."

"Usually she likes us to know what the charge—"

"Just get the dumb kid down to the station, okay?" Mr. Frederick said.

"Yup, yup," Mike Peders said.

Janice, who's a county prosecutor, decided I wouldn't get hit with criminal trespass, which could cause me a lot of problems. Mr. Frederick, Officer Peders, and Janice (don't remember her last name) talked in this conference room, and I was issued a misdemeanor citation for disorderly conduct, essentially amounting to disturbing the peace by setting off the alarms. Apparently they got a hold of Mr. Corrigan, and he was fine with that charge. It was all really great news.

Except for the part when Mr. Frederick said he wanted to talk to me and Dad in person. "Will Chuck be back in town over Thanksgiving?" he asked.

"Uh," I said. "Yeah, I guess."

"We need to have a sit down, Taco. All three of us."

That was bad because I'd been able to keep Dad in the dark about everything so far. I didn't like bothering him with drama. He'd gone through enough pain already in his life.

The other bad news was I had to pay a $177 fine and take off school in early December to go up to the circuit court in Lancaster to plead guilty or not guilty (when I surely was guilty of doing what they said) or to ask for the fine to be reduced since I didn't have any money.

Janice said if I pled not guilty, there'd actually be a trial! That sounded pretty cool in some ways. (Imagine me shouting, "You can't handle the truth!" at the judge.) But it also sounded really serious.

I didn't know what to do about the whole deal.

Anyway, no matter what, I count myself very fortunate. If the cops hadn't shown up, I could've been killed by that wooden Balinese chicken, scared into falling headfirst onto the birdbath below.

Darius picked me up from the cop shop after his shift at Captain Stabby's. It was midnight, and he was pissed.

"Dude," Darius said, driving me in his car, "this must stop. Please! I can't deal with this bullshit all the time. You know I made all kinds of promises about taking care of you, but I can't handle your shit! I can't handle my own shit! You stop or I'll be forced to kill you, okay?"

"You haven't told Dad about my trouble, have you?" I asked.

"He knows about your ass."

"I know that," I said. "What about the other stuff?"

"No, but he's going to find out you were arrested. It's going to be on the radio, I bet! People are going to talk, Taco!"

"But you haven't said anything about Maggie?"

Darius shook his head. "No. I'm not going to tell him. That's your responsibility. Hopefully he'll pitch in some cash to help figure out this mess."

"It's not a mess. It's a baby," I said.

Darius didn't say anything for a few seconds. He just

shook his head. Then out of no place, he screamed, "You have to get your head out of your ass, Taco!"

"I'm sorry, brother," I said.

We drove the last minute in silence, and Darius tromped off to bed without another word.

Get your head out of your ass, I thought.

Only later did I realize that I still had no idea where Maggie was.

CHAPTER 12

I spent the night refreshing my email, waiting for Maggie to message me, but she didn't. Eventually I dozed off on the keyboard. As the sun came poking through the windows, I stumbled down the hall to my bed. I probably slept three hours when the phone woke me up. I leapt out of bed. "Maggie!"

No.

It wasn't Maggie Corrigan calling to ease the suffering in my heart. It was Brad Schwartz.

"Hey. How's it hanging?" Brad asked. "Tough night?"

"Uh. Had some trouble with big blue."

"Cop trouble," Brad said.

"Girl trouble too," I said. "And this wood chicken thing."

"Bad."

"Yeah."

"I heard about the cop part on the radio this morning. You're a celebrity. Dad says you'd better keep your nose clean from now on or he won't be able to hire you back at the pool next summer."

"Man," I said, "it's already on the radio?"

"All over Facebook too. Sharma had to beg his parents to help you study. They were all like, 'Akilesh, you will not cavort with a known criminal.' He convinced them that you're still reeling from all the bad luck in your life and it would be shameful to let you down now though."

"His parents are nice," I said. "I'm a lucky guy."

"Can I bring over some food? My mom made a bunch of meatballs, and we have like forty sub sandwich buns. She said we have too much, so we need to get rid of some of it."

"Oh, hell yeah!" I said. "I love meatballs!" I felt so completely fortunate to have such good friends, dingus. But then I got confused because there was so much weighing heavy in my mind. "Wait. What's going on again?"

"Remember? We're going to study calc?" Brad said.

"Oh, right," I said. "When you coming by?"

"Noon," Brad said.

I spent the next hour leaving long messages on Maggie's phone, even though it was clearly off. I was starting to lose all hope, and then she called.

I picked up the landline to hear a very irate angel.

"You stop it, Taco!"

"Maggie? Are you okay? Where are you?"

"I'm in Ohio! I'm at my grandma's. I told you I was going."

"Oh," I said. "That sounds familiar."

"The cops called my dad last night."

"Yeah?" I said.

"And now me, Mary, and Missy are getting blown up!"

"What? With bombs?" I asked. That scared me, dingus.

"On stupid Facebook. Everybody's posting about you getting arrested for climbing the side of my house. What are you doing? You have to stop, Taco!"

"You didn't call me after your doctor's appointment," I said. "I was worried and couldn't get a hold of you. I thought something was wrong."

Maggie took a deep breath. I could hear her all the way from Ohio. "There *is* something wrong," Maggie whispered. "I'm pregnant."

"I know. That's not wrong. That just *is*."

"Oh, is it?" Maggie asked.

"Well, sure. That's what happens when you do it without protection, even if you're only doing it for recreational reasons," I said.

"Oh God," Maggie said.

"What?"

"What are we going to do?"

"What do you mean?" I asked.

"You're crazy."

"Me?" I said. "I'm not crazy."

"Yes, you're completely nuts. Why do you keep climbing my house?"

"To see you!"

"God, Taco," Maggie said quietly. There was a long pause, and then Maggie Corrigan said words I almost could not fathom. "If you don't fly right, I'm seriously going to break up with you."

"No," I whispered. "Break up?"

"I'll have no choice."

"No, that's not true! You have all the choice!"

"Fly right, Taco."

Then she hung up the phone.

Even though she hadn't broken up with me, her threat felt like a portent, like a parasite that would kill our love. I was upset, so I tried Maggie's mom's approach to coping and broke some plates. This woke up Darius, who flew up the stairs and screamed, "Stop wasting our resources!"

I gave him the finger.

He wrestled me to the ground.

I kicked him in the knee.

He pulled my arm behind my back and lifted me off the ground. Then he swung me around and punched me in the eye. My nose started to bleed too.

I was about to hit him with a lamp or a book when Brad and Sharma rang the doorbell.

Darius pushed past me and shouted, "I can't deal with you anymore!" and ran out of the house in his underpants.

We watched him streak along the front of the house and turn into the backyard.

"Wow," Brad said.

"Your current situation is highly unsustainable," Sharma said. "I think you should speak with your father."

I didn't know what to say.

"Dude," Brad said. "There's dried vomit on your carpet. Is that yours?"

"Darius," I said.

"Really. You'd better call your dad," he said.

"He'll be home Wednesday for Thanksgiving," I said. Then I remembered that Maggie would be gone all week in Ohio. "Oh shit. Oh no," I said.

Brad and Sharma stared at me for a moment. Then Brad said, "How about we focus on some high-end mathematics?"

"Good call, brother," Sharma said.

"Oh God," I whimpered.

Darius came back a few minutes later. He stared at us sitting around the table with our calc books open, me with a bunch of Kleenex jammed up my bleeding nose. He shivered. "It's cold out there."

"It is," Brad confirmed.

"Winter's on its way," Sharma said.

"Yeah," Darius said.

"I brought some meatballs and subs," Brad said. "I'll heat it all up in a bit. You want some of that?"

"Yeah. Thank you," Darius said really quietly.

Me? I didn't say anything to that rat-bastard brother of mine. He didn't get my eye bad enough to make it black. But I had a big bump on my forehead, and my damn nose wouldn't stop bleeding. Mom would be so mad at him.

She'd be so mad at me too.

CHAPTER 13

Nancy Miskinis. That's a pretty interesting name. The Miskinis part anyway.

Dad showed up on Thanksgiving morning (not Wednesday like he said). He came in the door, said, "Hi, boys," and then walked around the house, examining the state of things to make sure we weren't doing any damage.

He wasn't alone. He arrived with a red-haired lady named Nancy Miskinis. She wore a giant pink puffy sleeping bag for a coat. That's what it looked like—a sleeping bag with a hole cut in the bottom. And when she pulled that off, the sweetest perfume poured off of her. I liked her right away.

"You can call me Miz, boys," she said.

"Okay!" I said.

"That's quite a bruise on your head, Taco," Miz said.

I nodded. I smiled. Darius made a fugly face if ever there was one. Me, I was very happy to meet this Miz because I'm a happy guy.

You know what? I *was* happy. I'd had a pretty good couple of days. Everyone at school thought it was super fly that I was arrested for climbing my girlfriend's house again. They were all like, "Awesome, man! That's courageous. You're a Taco Grande with special hot sauce!"

Coach Johnson called me into his office and said I had better stop acting like such a phenomenal dumb ass or I'd find myself derailed for years. I appreciated that he cared.

Actually, Mr. Edwards, Mrs. Mullen, Ms. Tindall, Mr. Lecroy, and Dr. Evans all took time to have private meetings with me and said pretty much the same thing Coach Johnson said. They were all looking out for my future. They wanted to make sure my tomorrows were as great as today, right? They're all good people.

I totally aced my calc quiz on Monday too. Brad and Sharma had come over on Sunday to study more. If you do the work, pal, anything is possible.

The choir room was rife with kids singing *Wizard of Oz* songs, as auditions were the following week. Everyone was so nervous and excited about it all. I love the musical season! And Maggie was gone, so I joined right in.

Tuesday night had been the first home basketball game. Because I was cut from freshman b-ball—a stroke of luck that allowed me to go out for a musical, which

I love—I have been available to play the bass drum in the pep band during games. I'm not in band, but Ms. Carlson, the band director, says I have more pep in my step than anybody around. (That's true.) And holding down the beat is a fine way to show my enthusiasm for the team.

This home game was out of control too. Bluffton defeated Hazel Green by two points on a last-second three-pointer scored by Ryan Bennett. Everybody was falling over in the stands as the ball swooshed through the net. (I almost rolled over the bass drum.) Then we all rushed the court, and a bunch of people lifted Ryan over their heads. Hazel Green is like a tenth the size of Bluffton and only has six players, and we probably should've beat them by like a hundred points. But it was a wicked party at the end! Maggie wasn't there, seeing as she was in Ohio at her grandmother's, but that didn't ruin our victory. What a great day.

Wednesday, we didn't do work—not even in calc.

And then at eleven on Thanksgiving morning, Dad and Nancy Miskinis in her giant pink puffy sleeping bag walked in.

A few minutes after they arrived, after Dad's home inspection, Dad landed himself in the bathroom, which gave Darius an opening to start a conversation. He'd been staring at Miz like a confused caveman since they had arrived.

"Who the hell are you?" Darius asked her.

Miz smiled at him. Then she said, "Taco, help me bring in the food from the car."

"You got it!" I said.

We carried in a whole Thanksgiving dinner, pal. Turkey, stuffing, green bean casserole, mashed potatoes, cranberry sauce in cans, soft white bread, and two pies: one apple, one pumpkin. We had a feast on our hands, which made me like Miz even more.

The Detroit Lions started playing some football on TV, so Darius and Dad sunk into the couch and did what they do best, which is veg out (even though they both hate the Lions). I'm not about vegging, so I worked with the fragrant Miz to heat the beans, potatoes, and turkey.

"You're a little chef, aren't you?" Miz said.

"Well, I don't have formal training, ma'am, but I like to think I'm handy with a frying pan," I told her.

Darius seemed to think there was a wall between the kitchen and the living room, but there wasn't. Never was. He seemed to think me and the Miz wouldn't hear him behave like an animal.

"So is that our new mom?" Darius asked during a commercial break.

"No," Dad said. "You'll only ever have one mother."

"Are you doing her?" Darius asked.

"Darius," Dad said. "Careful."

"She looks like a portly pig in that coat."

"God damn it," Dad said. "You'd better put a cork in it."

"Or what? You'll have her sit on me?"

In the kitchen, like fifteen feet away from that hubbub, Miz smiled. "I think we can set the table. Is it easy enough to move your computer off there?"

"Yes, ma'am. It's no trouble at all," I said. I'm sure my face was red because I was so embarrassed about stupid Darius, but Miz seemed totally fine.

"Is porky serving us ham for dinner?" Darius asked.

"I'm sorry about him," I said to Miz. "Darius had a bad past life, so he's very ornery, generally speaking."

Miz winked at me. "I expected a little pushback. I suggested your daddy should let you both know I was coming, but he thought it would be a nice surprise."

"It sure is a nice surprise," I said.

"Aren't you sweet?" she replied.

Then she leaned over and gave me a grandma-style peck on the cheek. I could smell that perfume—or maybe it was lotion?—on my face the rest of the day. Whatever, dingus. I liked it a lot because mom types are good.

During the Thanksgiving meal, Darius stewed in his own sack of mad. He ate fast and hard and sort of growled while he chewed. I, on the other hand, made a lot of fine jokes, and Miz laughed and laughed and slapped my shoulder a bunch. Dad's eyes sparkled as he watched us make jokes. He clearly thought Miz and me were all that. I liked seeing Dad happy because he's not a very happy guy. Not normally.

Unfortunately, the good times couldn't last. The situation between Dad and me got tricky like two minutes after everybody ate their pie. Dad dropped his paper napkin on his plate and said, "Miz, Darius, how about you two go and finish watching the game? I need to have a conversation with Taco."

"About how he's gonna be a dad?" Darius hissed.

Dad's face turned red, and he shook his head.

"You going to talk dad to dad?" Darius taunted.

"Shut up," I told him. "You said you weren't going to tell him."

"How about you and me get to know each other over some football?" Miz said to Darius.

Darius kicked back his chair. "I'm going downstairs."

"You're welcome to stay for this discussion, ma'am," I said. Given what was about to go down, I really wanted her there to cushion the blow.

"I'm going to get a little beauty rest on the couch, I think." She smiled, but I could see the worry lines creasing her forehead underneath her big pile of red hair. "You boys do your talking."

A second later Dad said very quietly and slowly, "What the hell is Darius talking about?"

"Nothing," I said. "No biggie."

"There's shit going on, isn't there? Got a call from Mr. Frederick. Said he'd like to talk to the two of us over at Country Kitchen tomorrow. Said you got busted climbing up the Corrigan house again. Said he figured you had a crush on this crazy Maggie chick that you couldn't let go of. He laughed quite a bit about you, Taco. Laughed because he thinks you're such a good kid—just too enthusiastic."

"Uh-huh?" My heart was beginning to pound hard. "That's nice."

"Bullshit. You're a screwup. We don't have time or money for screwups in this family, do we?"

I wasn't sure if I was supposed to answer his question or not, so I said, "We should sit down and talk with Mr. Frederick, I guess."

Then Dad got even quieter. "Taco," he said. "What the hell does Darius mean dad to dad?"

My heart really took off right then, pal. It raced

so fast, it made me dizzy. I heard echoes of what Mr. Frederick said when the cops pulled me off the Corrigan home, what Mr. Corrigan said when Maggie and her mom were fighting. The words reverberated in my mind. *This is real. This is real. This is real.*

"Um. Well. Maggie Corrigan wanted to show that she loved me, and I love her completely, so we began to do it…recreationally."

"Do it recreationally?" Dad's face turned purple. "Where?"

"You know…in her woman parts."

"Yeah, no shit. Where did this 'doing it' take place?" Dad asked. "In her car? Out by Belmont Tower? The Big M?"

Oh balls, I didn't want to answer where. But I couldn't lie to Dad's face, and I couldn't just not talk. "Here," I said. "In the master suite."

Dad reached across the table and slapped my face. His thumb smacked the bruise from my fight with Darius, which made my eyes water really badly. "Why was there a girl in this house? I told you no girls."

I blinked because I couldn't see very well with the tears. "Because I love her and my butt hurt, so I felt like I had to bend the rules."

Dad slapped my face again. His wedding ring—the

one that made him married to mom, not Miz—stung my cheek.

"Shit. Don't," I said. "Please."

"You disobeyed me," Dad said.

"Yes," I said.

"And she's pregnant? Is that's what Darius meant?"

"Yes," I whispered.

"Goddamn it, goddamn it, goddamn it, Taco."

"I didn't mean it. We weren't trying."

"No shit. What is she going to do about it? Get rid of it?"

"I don't know." I blinked my tears. They rolled down my face. "I don't know anything," I said.

"Are you going to be on the hook for child support?"

"I…I don't really know what that means."

"Jesus Christ!" Dad shouted. He stood up. He kicked the computer tower, which was sitting in the corner of the room. "Miz!" he shouted. "I need some air. Let's walk."

Miz got up fast and hightailed it after Dad, who was stomping out the door. It was maybe forty degrees out there, but they didn't take their coats.

They disappeared down the street. I stood at the picture window and watched for them because I wanted to tell Dad I was sorry for breaking the rules and being such an idiot and everything.

While I was waiting, Darius came upstairs. "Don't worry about that asshole, man. He barely gives us any cash anyway. Every month it goes down by like fifty bucks. Pretty soon I bet he doesn't give us anything. This is our house, not his house."

"Really?" I asked.

"I paid the rent for November. All of it," Darius said. He puffed out his chest like a king or something. But he actually made me scared because I know Darius wasn't a king.

"Shit. I have to… I should get a job…you know, to help you out."

Darius shook his head. "You don't think I can take care of you?" he bellowed.

"There are expenses, Darius. You have expenses, and I have expenses. I have a fine to pay, you know? And there's Maggie."

Darius glared. He spoke really slowly. "That is not the deal. I work my ass off so you can be a kid, so you do well in school, so you do your stupid extracurriculars, so you graduate and go to college. You will not get a job, Taco, or all this torture you're putting me through is a total waste."

"But we're screwed," I said.

"I can handle it."

"But my fine? And Maggie?"

"I can handle your fine," Darius said.

"But the baby?"

"Shut up, Taco. You don't have a baby. Maggie Corrigan has a baby."

"No, asshole," I said. "I have a baby too. If I can't get a job, give me my damn swimming pool money so that I can afford my stupid life!"

"You tell Maggie Corrigan that she's not welcome in this house anymore. Not ever again or I'll call the cops. You got it?"

"You're a jerk!"

"I'm your dad!" he shouted back.

We both got quiet. Just then we heard a car start. Dad and Miz were back from their walk, but they didn't come inside. We watched them through the picture window. They just took off.

"What the hell?" I shouted. "Miz's sleeping-bag coat is in the closet!"

"They're probably going back to the hotel to drink."

"Why aren't they staying here?"

"Because Dad's an asshole. I'm sure they'll waddle their fat butts back soon enough though. Dad won't want to buy her a new coat," Darius said. Then he turned and went back down to his basement.

Dad didn't contact me for the rest of the day. Later he called Darius and invited him out.

"I'm going to meet the jerk over at Dieter's," Darius said. "He wants to discuss you."

"Why can't I go?" I asked.

"First, you're in high school. You can't go to a bar. Secondly, he doesn't want to talk *to* you—just wants to talk *about* you," Darius said.

I still figured Dad would swing by sometime during the evening to talk (and to get Miz's coat), but it didn't happen. Around 9:00 p.m., the phone bleated, but it wasn't Dad. Mr. Fredcrick was on the other end of the line.

"Hey there, Taco," he said.

"Yeah?" I asked. I couldn't get a lot of air because I was home alone and didn't know what the shit was going on with anyone.

"You and your dad are meeting me at Country Kitchen at 9:15 tomorrow morning."

"We are?" I asked.

"Your dad will pick you up at nine, okay?"

"Why didn't Dad tell me?" I asked. "Why are you calling?"

"He's a little stumped about your state of affairs, son. He didn't want to yell at you, so he asked me to make the arrangements."

"He probably didn't want to hit me either," I said.

"Hit you?" Mr. Frederick asked.

"Never mind," I said. "See you tomorrow."

I had a very shitty night.

CHAPTER 14

I was barely showered and dressed when Dad pulled up to the house. My eyes were hazy. I had the cold sweats, and my brain was only half present. I was a zombie boy.

It was a cold day. All the leaves were off the trees, and the wind blew hard. I didn't want Dad to come back into *my* house ever again, so I carried out Miz's fragrant coat to Dad's car. He had the heat on, which was nice. (I was surprised he even used heat. Wouldn't that affect his gas mileage, the cheap bastard?) I threw Miz's coat in the back seat. Dad grunted. He pulled away from the curb.

"You sleep okay?" he asked.

"Not at all," I said.

"Me either. Not a wink," he said. "Sorry I hit you."

"Yeah. Great. Thanks for that," I said.

Dad drove slowly, and he kept glancing at me. His eyes were wet. "I mean, really sorry," he said.

Shit. I couldn't stay pissed, which pissed me off. "I appreciate that, okay?"

Dad focused on the road. "But the fact remains you're in big trouble."

"Okay," I repeated, not sure what else I could say that would change the situation.

"I didn't tell Frederick about your pregnant girlfriend. He doesn't know," he said.

We rolled down the hill and took a right at the high school grounds. The Big M, this giant white M (M because the college was a mining school way back in the day) that college students built on a hill like a thousand years ago, hovered to our left. Then Dad hit the gas, and we shot across town to the strip on Business Highway 151, where there are a bunch of chain restaurants, including Country Kitchen.

Inside Country Kitchen, we found Mr. Frederick and an unexpected guest sitting with him at the table. It was Randy Nussbaum, this big-faced, round-bellied lawyer. I'd heard other people say he was a little crooked. But I'd always liked him. He always showed up at football games and basketball games. He was funny. Shouted funny stuff.

Dad shook hands with both men, and we sat down. Dad asked Mr. Frederick about Cody. Apparently UW—La Crosse had a play-off game against Whitewater the following day. Cody wouldn't start, but he might play because the starting quarterback had a sprained wrist.

While Dad and Mr. Frederick talked, I nodded at Randy Nussbaum. He smiled at me, sort of laughed. "You're sure shooting off like a Roman candle lately."

"Yeah," I said, but I wasn't sure what he meant.

Apparently Dad had heard his comment. "You don't even know the half of it," Dad mumbled.

"Let's get you guys some coffee. Hot chocolate, Taco?" Mr. Frederick asked.

"Yes, sir," I said.

After the waitress put our steamy mugs in front of us, Mr. Frederick said, "Randy and I've been talking about Taco's legal predicament. Disturbing the peace isn't the worst charge, but Taco's got a fine coming."

"Hundred and seventy-seven bucks," I said.

"Damn it." Dad shook his head.

"That should be the end of it," Nussbaum said.

"Except," Mr. Frederick continued, "Taco's a hell of a student. Listed in the honor roll every semester."

"Is that right?" Dad asked. He seemed surprised, which was dumb because it was in the paper. Mom used to cut out the rosters for honor roll and hang them on the refrigerator.

"Well, yeah," I said.

"Scholarship material. Elks, Jaycees, VFW, all the service organizations in town are liable to throw support behind a kid like Taco because of his—"

"Impoverishment," Dad said.

"More like his can-do attitude given your family's history," Nussbaum said.

"Uh-huh," Dad said.

"But, Chuck, I got to say, a blemish on his criminal record is likely to sway those scholarships toward someone else, someone maybe less deserving but who looks better on paper."

"Wait. Are you guys talking about college? College scholarships?" I asked.

"There are consequences for idiotic behavior," Dad said.

"Randy had a suggestion, but we wanted to discuss it with you, Chuck," Mr. Frederick said.

"What's that?" Dad asked.

"An internship," Nussbaum said. "Up at my office."

"For pay?" Dad asked.

"No, although I'd provide Taco's legal representation for free. I'd go up to Lancaster for court next week."

"Slave labor," Dad said.

"No, sir," Nussbaum said. "Experience. Taco'd have an opportunity to do some paralegal work, see how the judicial system functions. And we'd be able to tell the judge about the steps he's already taking to get his life back on track after his juvenile mistake. I bet we could get that fine reduced or dropped entirely."

"Oh yeah?" Dad said, seeming more interested in the idea. "No fine?"

"An internship would look good on his college applications too," Mr. Frederick added.

"I have my summer swimming pool money for college," I said. "I'd really like to go to college."

"You what?" Dad spat. "How much money?"

"I don't know. Darius takes care of it," I said.

"You're damn thieves," Dad whispered.

Mr. Frederick and Mr. Nussbaum stared at us.

Dad stared back for a few seconds with a grimace. Then he said, "Taco will do this internship of yours, Nussbaum. Thanks for looking out for him. We appreciate it."

"We know he's a good kid, Chuck," Nussbaum said.

"Cody adores him, Chuck," Mr. Frederick added.

"Yup," Dad said.

But I'll tell you this, dingus: Dad didn't seem to appreciate the complimentary feedback at all. He slid out of the booth, shook hands with Nussbaum, and then said to Mr. Frederick, "Hope Cody kicks Whitewater's ass tomorrow." Then he turned and walked out.

I slid over and stood. "Thanks, Mr. Nussbaum. Thanks, Mr. Frederick."

"No guarantee the judge will go for it, but I think he will," said Nussbaum.

"I don't have money to pay for my hot chocolate," I said.

Mr. Nussbaum smiled. "I'll take it out of your pay, Taco. You be ready to go to court Wednesday morning at 9:20. Got it? I'll swing by the school and pick you up. We'll ride over to Lancaster together."

"This is a good opportunity, Taco," Mr. Frederick said.

I thanked them both again, although I wasn't sure what it was I'd actually agreed to. Then I speed-walked to catch Dad at the car before he tore out of the Country Kitchen parking lot without me.

On the way back to the suite, Dad said, "Look what you make us do."

"What?" I asked. "What are we doing?"

"Accepting charity. They pity us."

"They're just being nice. They're good neighbors."

"Meanwhile you and Darius are hiding money and pretending you don't have enough for food," Dad said.

"No," I said. "Darius is protecting my future."

"Bullshit," Dad said. We didn't talk for the rest of the drive.

When Dad pulled his car in front of the suite, he had this final thing to say, "You'd goddamn better get it together, Taco. You make sure that girl has a plan for this baby that doesn't include you paying for it because unless you plan on dropping out and getting a real job, we can't afford it. I'm through digging you and Darius out of your messes. Do you understand? I have my own responsibilities."

"Fine," I said.

I got out of the car, but before I shut the door, I leaned back in. Dad's the only dad I'll ever have, right? "Listen. Why don't you come in for a few minutes?" I said. "We don't get to see much of you. Darius is kind of sad, you know? Kayla is getting married to some other dude. Did you know that?"

He didn't even answer the question. All he said was, "We got to get back north. We're taking Miz's daughter to dinner because we couldn't spend Thanksgiving with her."

"Are you and Miz married?" I asked.

Dad looked straight ahead. "Not yet," he said. "Take care of that thing with your girl."

I slammed the door as hard as I could, and the car shook. All I wanted was a little kindness. I'd be happy for Dad to tie the damn knot with a puffy-coat sack named Miz! But I got no kindness, only jerkiness!

Of course, then I felt bad. I called Dad's cell from the

suite later in the day and told him I was sorry for slamming the car door. I decided, no matter what, I should be happy he'd found new love.

He said, "Okay," and hung up.

CHAPTER 15

So the Wednesday after Thanksgiving, Darius wrote me a note to get me out of school.

Dear Whoever,

Taco has to go to court today. He's gotta leave after first hour. Maybe he'll be back later in the day, but maybe not. Please excuse his unexcused absence.

Darius Keller

A heaviness had settled in my heart. Maggie hadn't shown up on Monday or Tuesday. Did she stop loving me? Did she have an abortion? She hadn't called me or anything, so what was I to think?

But as I walked past the trophy cases on my way to meet Mr. Nussbaum out front of the school, there she was. Danielle Corrigan was dragging Maggie by the hand toward the office.

I stopped cold in my tracks, dingus. I couldn't move. My heart pounded in my throat.

Maggie saw me and stopped. "Taco!" she shouted.

"Maggie!" I cried.

Danielle gave her a big yank. "God. First person we see. Don't you look at him. Don't you speak to him. Let's go. Now."

Maggie stumbled forward and turned to wave at me as they rounded the corner, but she didn't say another word. I could tell she wanted to though. The time apart hadn't destroyed our love. No way! And holy nuts, pal, she looked thick and puffy in her face. Something—maybe the ghost of my mom—whispered in my ear, *The baby is still inside her.* And so I walked out the front door with huge pep in my step, a wind beneath my wings, and outside I found Randy Nussbaum waiting for me in his super fly Cadillac.

"Hey, hey!" he called from the open window. "It's the Taco!"

Lancaster is only like fifteen minutes away from Bluffton. You get to roll through these crazy deep valleys and up along these sweet ridges that let you see for miles and miles. All the corn was in, but a few black-and-white Holstein milk cows were out munching the frozen ground, so you could tell you were still in farm country.

I popped on Dad's old clip-on tie he used to wear to weddings and other festive/formal occasions.

"Looking good," Mr. Nussbaum said.

"I want to make a good impression," I said.

"I already chatted up Janice. She likes our plan. She's going to drop the charges at the arraignment."

"No fine?" I asked.

"You're lucky people like you so much. It's like every day is Taco Tuesday," Mr. Nussbaum said and smiled.

"It's Wednesday," I corrected him.

"True enough, Taco." Mr. Nussbaum smiled even bigger and nodded.

Dingus, you don't even know. At the courthouse people treated me so well. Everyone smiled like Nussbaum, and Janice, who is the prosecutor, shook my hand when she saw me.

There was also this other kid there about my age from Potosi. Instead of a sweet clip-on tie, he was wearing this giant Tweety Bird T-shirt about three sizes too big with the words *I tawt I taw a puddy!* on it, and his pants were all sagged, so his jean crotch was about at his knees. He had his turn with the judge right before me. Turns out he'd been charged with criminal trespassing for breaking into an old railroad car. He pled guilty, and the judge told him he was acting disrespectful, even though I didn't hear him say a word. Then he got a thousand-dollar fine and fifteen days at the county juvenile facility. *Holy nuts!*

I was up next. The judge smiled at me, so I figured we were off to a good start. Janice said she was recommending I go under the tutelage of Randy Nussbaum so I could better understand the legal system and make brighter decisions in the future. The judge said it all sounded like a good plan. "Keep getting those good grades and keep your nose clean, Mr. Keller," the judge said. "Your amygdala will catch up to your talents soon enough."

"Mr. Keller is my dad. Call me Taco," I said.

Everybody laughed. But I wasn't laughing. I just don't like being called Mr. Keller. To be totally honest, I was a little pissed at the judge for treating Tweety Bird so badly. Kid just did a little trespassing. But he had to go to jail and pay a huge fine? Where was Potosi's Mr. Nussbaum? Where was Potosi's Janice? Why couldn't Tweety work in a law office instead of getting locked up?

After court Mr. Nussbaum took me to Doolittle's, this bar and grill by the courthouse. He bought me a cheeseburger. While I munched, I asked Mr. Nussbaum why Tweety Bird had it so bad.

"Attitude is half the game, Taco. If you had shown up wearing a profane T-shirt and gangster pants, the judge wouldn't have treated you so well either."

"What if Tweety doesn't have a tie? What if he can't afford one?"

"You can't afford a tie, but you showed up in one, didn't you?" Mr. Nussbaum pointed out.

I shrugged.

On the drive home, I thought about ways I might break Tweety out of jail and how we could both run for the Canadian border. I didn't really want to go to Canada though, so I decided to stop thinking about it, mostly because I had more important things to deal with.

One, Maggie had returned. And two, I had my audition for the musical. (I hadn't canceled it because before that morning I thought Maggie might have left for good.) I considered humming a little to make sure I had the song ready, but I didn't want to annoy Mr. Nussbaum, so I sang in my head and looked out the window the rest of the way.

CHAPTER 16

I got back to school just in time to warm up for the tryouts. I was all set to sing a little bit from "The Merry Old Land of Oz," even though I can't really sing that great. (I'm probably the forty-second best singer in my class.)

When I arrived at school, however, a couple things went down that made me think maybe I should skip out on that whole shiz.

First, when he dropped me off, Mr. Nussbaum asked me to go to his office right after school on Friday. (It would've been Thursday, but he had to be in court.) "I want you to get rolling, Taco," he said. "We need to get a routine established." How could I be in the musical if I had to serve the law after school every day? I couldn't.

Secondly, Maggie Corrigan was not only back. She was standing by my locker when I got to school. I stopped in my tracks when I saw her.

"I've been looking for you all day," she said.

I approached slowly. It had been so long since we'd talked, and so much had happened. "You should be in class. You have to keep doing well in school," I said. "People think you're a good person—even if you're not—when you're good at school. You don't want to go to jail like Tweety Bird, do you?"

"Costume loft please," Maggie said.

That set me off. "Why? You want to get naked? No! That's a stupid idea! I'm not getting naked with you until after our baby comes and you've explained how you can go for a full week without calling or replying to my painful emails!"

"That's what I want to talk about! I don't want to take off my clothes, okay? I just want to go someplace private," she said. Then she pointed her finger in my chest. "Follow me. Now."

She moved like lightning, and I had to hurry to keep up with her.

But when we got to the stage area, the whole wide world of musical doink was standing on stage around the baby grand, belting out, "We're off to see the wizard!" so we couldn't go to the loft.

"Crap," Maggie said. Then she turned on her heel and shot out past the auto shop and the driver's ed room. We burst into the back parking lot, which was highly illegal, given how there was still ten minutes of school before the bell rang.

"Maggie, shit. What the hell are we doing?" I asked. "I'm already in trouble. I was at court today!"

"I'm in trouble too, which means we're in trouble together," she said.

"How?" I asked.

"My parents are totally harassing me, man." Maggie's lips were quivering. Tears began to fill her eyes. "I'm going to fold if they don't stop. Mom was hell on wheels in Ohio. Hell on wheels!"

"What do you mean 'fold'?"

"Abort the mission or…or sign up for adoption," she said.

"No," I said. "That can't happen. You're my family. You and the baby."

Maggie nodded. "You're my family too. That's why this happened, right? Because it was meant to? You're all I love."

"What can we do to stop them?" I asked.

"I have plan. But it's going to be tough." Maggie breathed out hard. Then she whispered, "We need to fake not being in love for a while because my mom has to believe that this is *my* decision, and in it we're not together."

"No," I said. "I can't do that." How could I do that? How could I not show my love?

"Shut up, Taco! You have no idea what I'm dealing with."

"But you're my *family*," I said.

Maggie paused. She was so serious. "If we don't fake this, they're going to come after you, okay? They'll probably come after you anyway, but maybe we can convince them they don't have to," Maggie whispered.

I squinted at Maggie. "Come after me? Like rough me up? Break my knees? Go gangster or something?"

"No. They want to pay you off," Maggie said. "Pay you to go away. With cash."

"No," I said. "No way."

"To get you to sign away your parental rights, they will bribe your ass big-time. They will try to pay you to stay away from me forever. Do you understand? That's how angry they are about what happened."

"What kind of person do they think I am?" I said, shocked by what the Corrigans were capable of. "My love is not for sale. I won't sell babies."

"Of course you won't. I hate my mom! And my dad! They're shitty, shitty people."

I felt like I'd been kicked in the salad, dingus. I stared at the pavement. "Why would they think I'd care about money more than a baby?"

"Because they think you're poor and depraved."

"Jesus," I whispered.

"I know better. I know you," Maggie said. "So here's the deal. Just pretend not to love me, and I'll pretend not to love you. And I'll have this baby, and then you… you come swooping in to be the dad. When I go into the hospital to have the baby—swoop! There you are. And then it will be too late because the baby will be there, and they can't just keep the dad away because they're the grandparents. They can't!"

Then Maggie said more quietly, "When they see the baby, maybe then they'll just be happy for me."

That sounded peaceful. That sounded like a good plan.

She got loud again. "And when we're married and living together as a family in your house, they won't know what hit them! Mom will shit her stupid pants! I will never let her see the baby! She will cry herself to sleep every night, and it will be her own fault!"

"Oh shit," I said. Our baby is a weapon? "Really?"

"She can hurt me," she said. "But I can hurt her more."

"But…but maybe we shouldn't lie. I want to see you," I said. "To help you. You know, to care for you when you're supercharged pregnant and stuff. I took care of my mom. I can take care of you too."

"No, man. The only way you can help right now is to work. I'm not going to be able to stay at Dairy Queen when I'm pushing maximum density this spring. That means we'll have no money unless you get a job. I'm already doing my job. I'm making life in my body, and soon people are going to know I'm pregnant. I'm going to get so much shit for this."

Maggie was all heated up, pretty much yelling, which was sort of normal for her, and I've always liked how engaged she was in her life, right? This was even better! It was like listening to one of Coach Johnson's wicked halftime speeches.

"I'm doing my damn part! Now you do yours!" Maggie shouted. She grabbed me by my white dress shirt collar. "You do it!"

"Okay. I'm in. In fact, I already tried to get a job. But apparently I'm not qualified to be a dance instructor."

That made her smile. She took a deep breath and sighed. "Just keep at it, cowboy," Maggie said. "You're so awesome. You really are, Taco. We're going to do this." Then she grabbed my ears, and she kissed me so hard, my pants tried to unbutton themselves. When she stopped, I was all dizzy, and she said, "I have to get to the locker room and change for cheerleading before everybody else gets there because you can see I have a baby bump if you look hard enough."

I looked. Maybe I could see it. A little. My baby in a baby bump. "I love you so much," I said.

"Shut up about that. No more," Maggie said, putting her finger to my lips. Then she left.

I hung out in the back lot for a few minutes, tucked behind a Dumpster, trying to compose myself. The bell rang while I was out there. A whole gang of guys, the car shop dudes, came pushing out the doors. A couple of them lit cigarettes. They were all like, *Taco! You're the man*, because those guys always say crap like that to me. But actually this time I felt like the man. Like a real man! Like a man who was about to get a real job and be a real dad. A manly man!

I high-fived a few of those car monkeys and shot back inside and cruised down the hall with my head held high. But when I neared the auditorium, Caitlin Krebs ran up to me and grabbed my hand. "We've been looking for you! You're up, Taco! It's your time!"

Five seconds later I was standing on stage in the bright lights next to Ms. Brogley, who played the piano. I sang "The Merry Old Land of Oz!" At the end, I spread my arms out wide and slid down into a split to show I really meant it. Mr. Lecroy, the choir director, shouted, "A little off-key but plenty of enthusiasm. And those moves! The boy can deliver! I think we've found our Mayor of Munchkinland!"

The kids who were watching the auditions clapped

and whooped. Caitlin Krebs flew from stage right and hugged me, pressing her boobs into me. I whooped too. I did because I was pumped! Mayor of Munchkinland? That's like playbill headliner material. I would have lines to say and everything. Mom would be so proud of me. Remember, dingus? She loved musicals. I was going to be the man for Maggie...and for Mr. Lecroy... and for Mom.

Except I wasn't the man. How could I be the munchkin mayor? I had to get a job for Maggie and the baby. And I had to go to Nussbaum's to do the law.

Oh man.

CHAPTER 17

On Friday morning, Mr. Lecroy gave a dramatic reading of the musical cast list over the intercom during announcements. This was a big surprise! I hadn't had a chance to tell Mr. Lecroy that it probably couldn't work out for me to be the mayor.

Maggie didn't sit next to me in English. I figured she was pretending not to be in love with me so that we could fool the world and surprise them when we got married. Our baby could be the best man in a little tux or the maid of honor in a poofy, lacy dress, but then after English out in the hallway, Maggie kicked my ass. She literally kicked me in the ass! Which inflamed my almost-healed coccyx, which I hadn't thought about in a few days, even during my split at musical tryouts.

Pain fired through my nether regions when her pink Chuck Taylor high-top made contact.

I cried out in pain.

"Shut up," Maggie hissed. "You're in the musical?"

"My ass!"

"Have you found a job?"

"It's only been a couple days since I knew I needed one."

"How are you going to get a job to support our..." Maggie got very quiet and looked around to see if anyone was looking at us. Of course, every damn monkey in the hallway was staring. She whispered, "To support our habit?"

"Our what?"

"Habit," Maggie said louder.

"Habit?"

Maggie just glared.

"Jesus. Leave it to me," I said. My ass hurt so much that I thought I was going to cry, and that jacked me up pretty hard. "You listen," I said with full-on frying anger because she had hurt my butt and my heart so badly, "You just watch me do my thing. Because I'll do it. But for now I'm going to calc."

As I limped through the halls, I thought about how my dad wasn't interested in anything except football and beer and how I liked football and dancing and musicals and track and how lucky that baby was to have such a well-rounded dad. Maggie could suck it because I could handle all my responsibilities, and I would do all these activities because my baby deserved awesomeness for a role model.

I got to calc, like, two minutes late, and Mr. Edwards's eyeballs shot daggers at me while he finished giving instructions for working on a problem set. My ass was throbbing so much that I could hardly concentrate.

While we were supposed to be working, Brad Schwartz leaned over. "Are you on drugs? You and Maggie? That would explain a lot to be honest."

"What?" I asked.

"Katie Faherty texted me because she heard you have a habit."

"Mr. Schwartz, Mr. Keller, please shut your mouths," Mr. Edwards said.

"My dad's Mr. Keller!" I shouted. "Call me Taco!"

Mr. Edwards was not pleased by my clarification. He told me to stand in the hall for ten minutes to get my shiz under control. I saw a couple teachers I liked while I was out there and said hi to them, which made me think about how those same teachers wouldn't say hello to Maggie because she was not friendly like I was. Clearly it was another indication that I was a good person and not her. Why would I have such feelings about the girl I love? My ass killed.

And, yes, dingus, I was pissed at Maggie. And now everyone thought we had a "habit," and I was supposed to go to Nussbaum's law office after school at the same time I was supposed to be at the first musical practice. I'm a good person but not capable of time travel or being in two places at one time.

Plus, my ass hurt.

I am a lucky Taco though. That first day of musical practice was just an organizational meeting that only took like twenty minutes. Mr. Lecroy handed out a schedule of rehearsals that began the following Monday and ran right up to Christmas break (with a few optional meetings during the break) and through early February, when we would perform the musical for two weekends in front of God and Bluffton and also the kids in middle school.

During December, as Mayor of Munchkinland, I'd only have to be at rehearsal a couple times a week. Finding a job? Doing my young lawyering? Seemed sort of possible if I could slide getting a job past Darius without him punching my nose. I'd deal with January when January happened. I had a primo role, so I had to figure it out.

Thank God Sharma was just leaving the building as I was because my ass was grass from Maggie's foot, and the notion of hoofing two miles downtown to Mr. Nussbaum's law office nearly knocked me back on my ass. Sharma drove me in his brand-new Honda Civic.

On the way he asked, "What are you two junkies for?

Methamphetamine? That would make sense given your oddly energetic behavior. You certainly don't seem the barbiturate type."

"Who?" I asked. "What?"

"You and Maggie Corrigan, meth heads. You know, because you're drug addicts."

Oh, I wanted to tell Sharma the whole truth and nothing but the truth, so help me God, but I'd promised Maggie I'd keep a lid on the baby, so I lied. "Yeah, we're total meth fiends. I'm learning to cook it too."

"I can't tell my parents. They won't let me help you with calc anymore."

"No, don't. It's better they don't know," I said. Oh, I hate lying, dingus, but shouldn't Sharma know better? Did I look like a meth head?

Three minutes later we were on Main Street, and Sharma dropped me off at the Nussbaum Law Office. He asked if Nussbaum was helping Maggie and if I launder our money to avoid prosecution. I told him Nussbaum didn't know about our drugs or our production capacity.

Sharma is a bright dude generally. How could he buy all this *we take drugs* crap?

"I'm here for you if you need help," he said. "I can give you a ride to rehab anytime."

"Thanks for the ride," I said.

Then into Nussbaum's I limped. His office was up above Pancho Steinberg's Mexi-Deli, and I had to climb a long flight of stairs to get there. Never let anyone tell you your butt is not important. Your butt is very, very important to general motility.

Mr. Nussbaum's office had dark wood-paneled walls like a TV law office from the olden days. The first room had a reception area where there was a little desk with fake flowers and pictures of babies on it. No one sat there. I stood in that room for a few seconds and then called out, "Halooo?"

"Hey, hey! Taco!" The Nussbaum voice called from another room. (There were two doors—one on the right of the reception desk and one on the left.) "Come on back here!" he called.

I wasn't sure where his Nussbaum voice was coming from, so I tried the door on the left. The room was dark and smelled like old paper, coffee, and cigars. This, I was to find out, was the file room, which included a coffee station where I would make coffee after I uncovered the coffeemaker, which was buried in unfiled paper—just like the floor and everything else. I shut that door and hobbled around the desk to the door on the right. That was where I found a shirtless, big-bellied Mr. Nussbaum.

"You made it!" he shouted. He sat behind a huge

wood desk. There were two leather chairs across from him—leather chairs waiting for clients who would talk serious law business with him.

"You're naked!" I shouted back.

"I have on pants!" he shouted. "Gets so hot in this room that I sweat through my shirts. So I work like this…unless there's mixed company around."

"Is your receptionist gone for the day?"

"Mallory? She's gone for three months. She had a baby right before Thanksgiving. By statute I only have to pay her for six weeks though, so I got that going for me."

"Yeah. Righteous," I said.

"Sit down here. Let's have a chat, Taco."

I eased myself into one of the leather chairs, and my coccyx nestled in the most delicious leather cloud an ass might ever find.

"What a chair!"

"Yeah. Nice, right? These are the spoils of war, my friend."

I nodded and smiled, though I had no idea what he meant, and Mr. Nussbaum took off at the mouth.

"Taco, I'm a small business man. I wouldn't do a public service just out of the kindness of my heart. You understand?"

"Yeah?" I didn't though.

"Good. Just so we're straight on the matter. You're not going to be dinking around here, flirting with my secretary. No, sir. You're going to put your nose to the grindstone. You're going to be my secretary. Got that?"

"Yes. Completely," I said.

"This is a real job, amigo. You will make me coffee on Saturday mornings while I am working. You will run out to get me dinner if I'm working late on a weekday. You will file the reams of paper I get buried under every single day. If you're smart, you'll photocopy cases, read them, highlight important information. And last but not least, you will make this office sparkle—and not just with your personality but with sponges, soap, the vacuum cleaner, and elbow grease. *Comprende?*"

"*Claro que sí,*" I said. But oh my, I wasn't even sure I knew what I'd just said. "You know I have to go to school, right?" I asked.

"Of course! We're on the same page, amigo," Mr. Nussbaum said. "Now let's get to the business at hand."

Mr. Nussbaum stood, took two steps to his left, and pulled a shirt off his coatrack. He pulled that puppy around his shoulders and strode across the room, through the reception area, and over to the paper/coffee/cigar room I'd poked my head into when I had first arrived. To follow Mr. Nussbaum, I'd had to jack myself out of that comfortable seat, and my ass didn't agree to this sudden movement. Mr. Nussbaum shouted, "Get the lead out, Taco! Catch up!"

In the coffee room, Mr. Nussbaum flipped on the light—and what an amazing, amazing sight. Paper was everywhere—all over the floor, piled in stacks against the walls, covering the tops of the filing cabinets, jammed underneath the coffeemaker. Everywhere there could be paper, by God, there was paper. You could get buried alive in a room like that.

"Your first task, amigo? Get these documents organized and filed," Mr. Nussbaum said.

"Organized how?" I asked. "Alphabetically?"

Mr. Nussbaum patted me on the shoulder. "I don't know, son. I'm the lawyer, not the filer. Mallory was out on bed rest before she had her baby, so this is a good two months of paperwork to sort out. You're going to figure out what the hell's gone wrong in this place…because wrong it has gone. Any questions?"

"No. Got it," I said.

"You are to put in twenty hours a week from now until the middle of February, when Mallory gets back. I want you here after school for a few hours every day and Saturdays for a minimum of eight hours. We'll have to work some Sundays, but not all. By February, you'll be a free boy. Fair?"

"When am I going to learn about the law?" I asked.

Mr. Nussbaum gestured to the mad stacks of paper. "The majesty of the law surrounds you."

"What about musical rehearsals?"

Mr. Nussbaum squinted at me. "What musical rehearsals?"

"The school's musical. I'm the Mayor of Munchkinland."

"And I'm the Fresh Prince of your Freedom. You'd better figure it out. Now you might not understand responsibility, given that home situation of yours, but this…" Mr. Nussbaum gestured to the papers again. "This is your primary concern for the next few months… or else."

"Or else?"

"Right. Or else," Mr. Nussbaum said. He pointed at me and winked. Then he said, "I'm going to the VFW for a beer. Make sure the door's locked when you go."

"I don't have keys."

"I'll leave you a set on Mallory's desk."

Mr. Nussbaum was gone in a blink, and I was left with this mountain of paper. If I could've gotten to the file drawers without stepping on paper, I'd have tried to figure out how all this "majesty of the law" was organized. But I couldn't walk anywhere without stepping on paper.

So I went out to the reception area, locked the door, lay down on the floor, and took a well-deserved nap. My ass sure hurt from Maggie's mighty kick. Pain is exhausting.

When I woke up, it was pitch-dark, and I could hear drunk college kids screaming on Main Street.

It was 9:00 p.m. I spent the next hour just making neat stacks out of all the paper. From what I could see, this was important stuff. Like printed emails from judges and other lawyers and clients and crap. There were documents from actual court cases. Judgments and divorce decrees and lawsuits. Holy shiz. I didn't actually file anything, but by the end of the hour, I'd made a path from the door to the cabinets.

Then I got seriously groggy. I had to call it a day.

I shut off the light and locked the door behind me. There was no light to show me where the stairs down to the street were, no light coming from any offices at the other end of the hallway. I couldn't hear anything either, no noise from the street. It was like I'd been buried underground, though I was above ground. Dingus, I totally froze.

"Mom," I said to nobody. "Help."

A door creaked in the dark. I fumbled, bumbled, stumbled toward the stairs. I felt like someone was behind me. I found the stairs and scrambled down as fast as I could. I burst out to the cold street, which was lit with streetlights and loud with screaming sorority girls.

Whoa, dingus. Even in their puffy winter coats, you could totally tell how hot these girls were.

Even if I didn't love all the piles of paper, I did love Nussbaum's office location!

I love life.

CHAPTER 18

The phone bleated at 7:00 a.m. on Saturday morning. I had been asleep, but I was worried enough about Maggie to zombie roll out of bed and answer. It wasn't my lady friend. It was Mr. Nussbaum. "Would you like a ride to the office, amigo?" he asked.

"You bet your pants," I said, although I wasn't exactly sure what was going on because I was still half asleep.

"I'll be at your pad in ten minutes," he said.

"My pad," I repeated.

I hung up the phone and crawled back into bed. Except instead of drifting back to dreamland, I sat up. This was real. This was not a dream. It was 7:00 a.m., and Mr. Nussbaum was just minutes away from the suite. I don't remember getting dressed. I don't remember brushing my teeth, but I'm sure I did. Fresh breath was a priority for this guy. The next thing I knew, I was riding in Mr. Nussbaum's fine Caddie, and we were cruising to do some law.

"You ready for action?" Mr. Nussbaum asked.

"Going to put a dent in those files for sure," I said, wishing I was still putting a dent in my pillow.

"Not today you're not. Saturday's my busiest day. We have a full docket of clients coming in. You'll need to meet and greet them, run in some coffee periodically, and maybe run out for some rolls or a sandwich or two. Today you'll be my face, my feet, and my hands."

I looked at my hand and said, "You are Mr. Nussbaum's hand."

"Ha-ha!" Mr. Nussbaum shouted. He's a peppy guy.

Mr. Nussbaum parked behind the building a half block off Main Street in front of a sign that read, "Da Hound Dog." Underneath in smaller letters, it said in parentheses, "(Nussbaum's Spot, Not Yours, Unless You Want to Get Your Butt Bit.)"

"You like my sign?" he asked. "Mallory got it for me last Christmas. She is a funny one."

"Whacky," I said.

Mr. Nussbaum slapped my thigh. "You're getting to know all about the world of Nussbaum, aren't you?"

The hall outside his office wasn't nearly as scary in the daylight, although I took note of some major-league spiderwebs in the corners. Mr. Nussbaum opened the office door, and in we went. He headed directly for the majesty of the law file room, and I got a little scared because I hadn't really done anything other than make piles. But he wasn't mad at all. In fact, Nussbaum was the exact opposite of mad.

"Taco! Aren't you an industrious fellow. Were you here all night?"

"Well, until past ten," I said.

Mr. Nussbaum's eyes got kind of moist. "Everybody told me you're a great kid." He began to nod. "Now I know it's true. This…" He gestured to the majesty of my stacks of papers. "This would've taken Mallory a week or more."

In my hour of labor the night before, I had unburdened the coffeemaker from also serving as a bookshelf for more paper. The thing was killer gross, pal. It was moldy and musty, but Mr. Nussbaum showed me where the cleaning supplies were, and I cleaned the coffeemaker. Now it wouldn't kill someone who had coffee from it. Then he showed me how to make coffee.

Four minutes later, coffee brewing, me seated at the reception desk (on a leather chair for maximum coccyx comfort), Nussbaum's first client arrived. Mr. Thomas Wrightman was a gristly seventy-three-year-old dude in dirty khaki pants that were falling off his skinny butt. Wrightman was suing his neighbor because the neighbor's dog would pee in Wrightman's yard so much that his grass, which he loved, started turning brown in patches.

It was a cold December, and all of Bluffton's grass was brown at that point. But I wanted to show my support. "That's a crime!" I commiserated.

"I will be compensated for my loss!" Wrightman cried.

"Big-time!" I said. "Stacks of cash!"

Mr. Wrightman smiled at me. He told me that I was not as pretty as Mallory but a whole lot more fun to talk to.

Every half hour another client visited. It turns out that the majesty of the law mostly involves resolving fights with neighbors, fights between business partners, fights that cause divorces (affairs and money and bad personal hygiene), and people who drink too much and do dumb things, ranging from running over stop signs in their cars to throwing rocks through their neighbors' windows. Fantastic!

I checked in the sad sacks, made small monkey chatter, brewed pot after pot of coffee, bought some sandwiches, ate a sandwich or two, played with a little kid whose mom was after cash from his deadbeat dad. The day rolled by fast.

About dinnertime Mr. Nussbaum shook hands with his last client (college kid who'd whipped rocks through a window) and escorted the sap to the door. Then he turned to me and said, "I got several positive comments about the work you did today, amigo. You're just what this office needs. A little ray of sunshine, aren't you?"

"Every day is the best day I ever had," I pointed out.

Mr. Nussbaum laughed. He didn't drive me home though. He had to go to the VFW to play some cards. That was a cold-ass walk in the Wisconsin December air, but I felt pretty good. Pretty damn great actually. I felt as if I brought a lot to the table, mostly because Mr. Nussbaum said I brought a lot to the table.

A talented and friendly fellow like me was certain to find work that could support Maggie Corrigan and my baby, right?

CHAPTER 19

I had the weirdest dream, dingus. Maggie and I were naked and leaping from rock to rock on the side of this really steep mountain. We were having fun, and when we'd land on the same rock, we'd totally make out. The valley below us was super green with all kinds of plants and flowers, and there were rabbits wearing those pointy hats you see Vietnamese people wearing in pictures about the Vietnam War. But these had ear holes that let their rabbit ears stick through. Everybody was laughing—all the animals and me and Maggie.

But then there was a crack in the sky, and dark ink started rushing through. The rabbits began to cry, and the plants started wilting. Maggie almost fell off her rock, but I caught her.

And then the Tibet baby (a baby that showed up in my dreams a lot and who might be my mom) floated up the hill, wearing shiny pants and a red hat. The baby motioned for us to follow it like it was trying to save us.

"Keep it away!" screamed Maggie. She swung at it, throwing us both off balance.

The Tibet baby hovered just out of reach. Tears started pouring down the baby's face.

Maggie screamed. "Eat shit, Mom!"

The baby screeched back like a parrot, "What about Darius? What about Darius?" and then Maggie and I fell into blackness.

Oh, dingus! Crazy, right?

I woke up soaked in sweat. This dream stressed me out so bad! *What about Darius?* I rolled out of the muck and stumbled through the dark hall to the top of the stairs. "Darius! You awake? Darius?"

There was no reply.

I stumbled down the stairs into Darius's stink pad, flipped on the lights, but found no Darius in his bed. Because I had a huge burst of adrenaline, I ran up the stairs to see if maybe he'd passed out on the couch, as he'd been doing lately after his late shift at Captain Stabby's, but he wasn't there. I opened the door to see if maybe he was a frozen corpse in the yard, but he wasn't in the yard. And his car was nowhere to be seen. Since he started driving again after his license revocation, he always parked in the street in front of the house because all our extra stuff from the mullet house was jammed into the garage. Darius wasn't home.

I ran into the kitchen to look at the clock I'd set above the stove. It said 3:11 a.m. The dead hour. Where was Darius?

Could there be a girl? I wondered. Maybe he found a sweet and loving replacement for Kayla.

No, not likely. He'd gone totally antisocial. He wouldn't talk to girls.

Would he be at a coworker's house, drinking a couple brewskis while jamming some video game? Maybe.

When he was in high school, Darius had a pack of friends he stayed out with all night long. But they had all left for college, and Darius stayed for tech school and to help with Mom. And then to help me after Mom died.

What about Darius?

I called his cell phone, but it went straight to voice mail. Then I lay down on the hall floor.

At 4:00 a.m., the suite phone made its lonely bleat.

I jumped off the floor and picked up in a blink. "Darius?"

"No, Nancy Goebel down at the police station."

"What?"

"Is your papa home?" Nancy Goebel asked.

"My dad is at his new life," I said.

"Oh," Nancy Goebel said.

"Is this about Darius Keller?" I asked.

"Yes, it is."

"I'm all Darius has got family-wise," I said.

"Oh? Okay then. Darius is at Southwest Municipal because he crashed his car into the KFC/Taco Bell."

"Oh no. Oh no," I whispered.

"Now he wasn't going real fast, and he only sustained minor injuries. But Officer Peders determined from a general smell test that Darius imbibed quite a few alcoholic beverages, so there are legal charges pending."

"How many?"

"Quite a few. Lots of damage at the drive-through window."

"Oh no," I said. "We can't have any more disasters."

"I'm real sorry. We'll bring him back over to the station in the morning." And with that, Nancy Goebel hung up.

I thought about calling Dad to ask him to come home or calling Brad or Sharma for a ride to the hospital, but I decided I'd better just do the best I could. Mr. Nussbaum had said just a few hours earlier that I brought a lot to the table.

Bring what you got. Show Darius you care.

I pulled on my coat and headed west on Kase Street. The hospital was only about a mile away on the other side of Smith Park. I would go there and show Darius I cared with my presence, even though he's a dumb ass and a danger to himself and others and also a criminal.

Boy hell howdy, dingus. That 4:00 a.m. December air cut right through my layers and froze my dolphin body stiff as can be. It took me more than twenty minutes to get to the hospital. And then it wasn't open! Not the regular doors anyway. The front entrance that we always went through when Mom was first sick was totally dark and completely locked. (When she got worse, she ended up in Madison, which has a great hospital.) I yanked and screamed at the door in case there was some kind of password I didn't know about since I was not an adult.

Southwest Municipal is tiny, and all the rooms are on the ground level, so I thought maybe I could find Darius's room if I went window to window and looked inside. Seemed like a good idea. Problem was that the curtains were closed in most of the rooms. *Just knock.* I almost started to, but then I worried how old farts with bad hearts might keel over dead if somebody *knock-knocked* on the window in the middle of the night. Might think the grim reaper had come to take them home. Not a good plan.

I was completely shivering at that juncture. Totally chattering my bones. So I walked around the block to generate a little warmth and to scout for Dumpsters I might use to climb up to the roof so I could slide in through an exhaust vent or something.

Boom! There it was, pal! On the opposite side of the normal entrance to the hospital, I found the *emergency* entrance. What I thought was the back of the hospital was really another front of the building! The emergency entrance was lit up like Christmas with a bright red sign and all kinds of florescent lights.

"Woo! Yes!" I shouted and ran to it as fast as I could because my shivering was ridonculous and likely bordered on deadly.

I shot through the double-wide automatic doors into an entryway pumped thick with sweet heat. I stood there for a few seconds to let that business seep in. The nurse or whatever stared at me from behind a reception desk. But it wasn't a nurse, because after I blinked a bit and my eyeballs unfroze, I realized it was Emily Cook, a cello geek from school, a senior.

"Hi, Taco. I've been watching you on all the security cameras. Are you casing the joint?"

"I was thinking about breaking in through the roof," I said.

"That doesn't sound feasible."

"You gotta do what you gotta do. I want to see my brother. I need him to know someone cares."

"You care," Emily said.

"Precisely," I said.

"That's really nice. But you can't see him," Emily said. "We're not open for visitors until 8:00 a.m."

"You could just let me go in," I suggested.

"Behind those doors." Emily pointed to these gray doors to her left. "You'll find a doctor and a couple nurses checking on patients. And you'll find a giant orderly who used to wrestle for the college. If a visitor goes back there during non-visiting hours, the orderly's job is to tackle the visitor and handcuff him to a wheelchair. So I can't let you go."

"Oh," I said. "I don't appreciate violence." I looked past her at the door, behind which my bro lay bent and broken.

Emily shook her head. "Me either. Violence sucks." Emily didn't say anything for few seconds. "You look frozen. Do you want some hot chocolate?"

I was trying to figure out how to make a dash for it, get past that wrestler to Darius, but hot chocolate sounded pretty good. "Maybe," I said. "Is Darius okay?"

"He was really, really drunk, but he wasn't hurt in the crash," Emily said.

"He has O+ and A- blood, which makes him seem drunker than he is," I explained.

Emily blinked at me a couple times. "There's no such thing as O+ and A- blood."

"No, there is," I said.

"No. Really. There's no such thing. Somebody's giving you a line. His blood alcohol level was .36, which is so far above the legal limit, it's, like, legally dead. Darius was drunk. Straight-up drunk. Way crazy drunk. He has big problems."

I smiled because Emily was being serious and straight, and those kinds of people remind me of my mom. "You're pretty smart. I like that a lot."

Emily smiled at me, big and pretty, like a goddess, which only happens when really serious people smile because it's such an awesome surprise. "Thanks, Taco," she said.

"I'll take that hot chocolate if the offer's still good."

Ten minutes later I was warm and dead asleep on a little love seat in the waiting room. Emily must've put a blanket on me, which made me cozy. I slept for an hour or so. Then all hell broke loose.

A ringing phone woke me up. Emily spoke. She said, "Yes. Oh no. Okay. We'll be ready." Emily stood.

I sat up. "What?"

"Sorority girl," Emily said. She turned and went through the door into the actual emergency room. Like twenty seconds later, an ambulance came screaming up to the doors. The paramedics pulled a girl on a gurney out of the back. She screamed. I could hear her screaming through the doors. Emily burst back into the room, followed by a nurse and a doctor. They tore past me and met the paramedics, who rolled the screaming girl inside.

"She's on something. Can't calm her down. Fell through the picture window at her house," a paramedic said.

The girl bled through gauze on her face and hands. She screamed, "My heart! My heart! Help me!"

The doctor said, "Shh, honey. We're going to take care of you. Nurse, prick her."

The girl screamed more. And she wriggled a ton.

"She wasn't freaking out in the ambulance like this," a paramedic said. "Relax, Dana."

"Got to quiet down, sweetie, or we can't help you," the nurse said.

That girl didn't quiet down a bit. She wriggled so hard. She was clearly trying to jump off the gurney, and the wrestler-orderly had to hold her down. The girl screamed more. I walked closer. The girl cried. I walked closer. Then the girl focused on me because I was standing very close at that point, my mouth hanging open. Her mouth dropped open too, and she started saying, "You're here!

You're here! Thank you for being here!" She smiled and cried at the same time.

The nurse said, "Can you relax, Dana? He's here, right?"

"You're doing great," I said. "You're okay."

She said, "I'm so glad you're here."

"You know it. I wouldn't be anyplace else," I said.

The girl totally stopped the wriggle, dingus. She relaxed. The nurse jacked her with a needle. The girl smiled at me and whispered, "Thank you." Then she went to sleep.

"What the hell was that?" the doctor asked.

The nurse shrugged.

One paramedic said, "Can you get Dana a bed so we can go?"

"Yep, yep," said the doctor.

They all rolled the girl in back. A few minutes later, the paramedics came back with their stretcher.

"Nice work, pal," one said to me.

"Who are you?" the other asked.

"Taco," I said.

"Sounds about right," the first one said. Then they left.

I sat down and stared at my reflection in the window. "I'm here," I said. It was beginning to get light. Morning.

Emily came back out a few minutes later. "Magical Taco."

"Is it eight yet?" I asked. "Time to see Darius?"

"No. But you can come in back if you want. Everybody's pretty impressed with you."

Emily motioned for me to follow her. I scurried after. She pointed me to a room. "He's in there. Probably not feeling too good. Take it easy on him."

I nodded and went in.

Darius was hooked up to an IV. That scared me because Mom always got hooked up to that shiz. Darius, who was awake, looked at me and shook his head.

"What's in there?" I asked, pointing at the IV bag.

"Go away," Darius mumbled.

"Are you dying? Are they not telling me the truth?"

"They're rehydrating me. That's all. Go away," Darius said.

"Why are you dehydrated? Did you sweat because you were running from the cops?"

"I would've run, but I was passed out. Leave me alone, Taco."

"No," I said. "I'm here because I care."

"Well, I don't," Darius said.

"That's not the point. I'm scared, and I love you."

"Aw shit," Darius said. Then he started crying. "Would you please go away?"

"No. What happened?" I asked.

"I'm stuck," Darius said. "I'm lost in here." He pointed at his heart.

"Oh," I said. "Yeah, I know what you mean. I think that can happen."

"I don't like it," he whispered.

"We're going to be okay," I said.

I sat there in his room, and Darius fell back asleep. I guess I fell asleep too. I think I dreamed about that Tibet baby again, and I was definitely startled when there was a knock on the door.

"What?" Darius sat up fast. "Ow! Ow! My head is breaking." He put his hands to his head, which pulled out his IV. Blood started running from his arm. "Aw shit!"

I jumped up, grabbed cotton balls that were sitting in a dish on a rolling table next to him, and applied pressure to the blood spout.

Mr. Frederick poked his head in the door. "Do you need me to get a nurse?" he asked.

"Hi, there!" I said. "Nurse would be great!"

Turns out Mr. Frederick wasn't there to be a pal. He had come on official duty. After the nurse cleaned up Darius, Mr. Frederick told him to get dressed. Darius did what he was told. Then Mr. Frederick cuffed him and took him downtown to the police station for processing. (It doesn't have anything to do with food processing by the way. I know because I asked when I was arrested.)

I couldn't go with Darius. Mr. Frederick said that they'd give me a call when I could pick him up and that it might be a good idea to get a hold of my dad. *Fantastic.*

You know who's nice? Emily Cook. She finished her shift a little before Darius got hauled down to the cop shop, but she waited for me. "I figured you might need a ride home. It's very cold out there."

"Thank you," I said. "You're incredibly nice."

She smiled that crazy big smile. Then she drove me home.

CHAPTER 20

Maggie called early in the morning.

"Holy crap, Taco. Carrie Cramer just texted me. She heard about Darius on Snapchat. Everybody's posting crazy pictures. He crashed into Taco Bell? Is he okay? People think he hit Taco Bell because he was mad at you. Is he at home? Are you safe?"

"He didn't just hit the Taco Bell," I told her. "Also KFC."

"I don't think you should be splitting hairs. I'm scared. I love you!"

"Shh. Don't say that. What if your parents hear?" I said.

"Everybody is out getting a Christmas tree at Piggly Wiggly."

"Listen, I don't think Darius was trying to kill me. I think he fell asleep because his blood is bad…or because he was so super drunk. Emily Cook said his blood problem is fake."

"Emily Cook?" Maggie asked.

"She was at the hospital. She's super nice," I said. "She drove me home."

"Emily Cook?" Maggie asked again.

"Yeah. Emily Cook."

"I'm going to try to come see you today," Maggie said. "I need to see that you're okay."

"See me? Okay," I said.

But Maggie had already hung up.

Since I was awake, I called Dad. My heart pounded. The call went to voice mail. I left a message. "You maybe heard. Darius got in some trouble overnight."

I sort of expected Dad to call right back, but he didn't.

Then I lay down in my bed and tried to read an essay for English. It was something about the proper way to choose a persuasive paper topic, but I think I read three words before my head crashed back into my pillow. I must've slept for hours because it was midafternoon by the time my eyes opened again. I probably would've slept until dark, but a noise woke me up. There was someone in the house. The floors creaked with footsteps. The cupboards in the kitchen opened and shut. Water ran in the sink.

"Maggie?" I asked.

"No, dumb ass."

"Darius?" I called. "The cops were supposed to call me. They set you free?"

"Yeah. But not for long!" Darius shouted. I heard him shuffle down the hallway to the suite. He pushed open my door and stared at me. He was so pale, pal. He had dark circles under his eyes. He seemed like he'd dropped about twenty pounds because his shirt looked too big and his pants were all dirty and baggy. "I'm going to jail. Prison. Like for real. Probably for all of January."

Oh man, I don't like anyone to feel bad, right? Much less my bro. It wasn't easy, but I tried to be positive. "Hey. No problem! You'll get your shiz straightened out there. Have a little time to think and reflect. I could probably use a little jail time myself. Really couldn't come at a better time in your life, you know? Figure out a path forward. Get your insides unstuck! This is perfect!"

"No, dude. Nothing about this is perfect," Darius said.

"Aw, come on. Everything's looking up."

"I've got fines. Big ones. I don't have car insurance either, so what about all that damage I did at Taco Bell?"

"Not just Taco Bell. KFC too," I reminded him.

"Yeah, Taco. I know, okay?"

I squinted at Darius. Something didn't compute. "Wait. You don't have car insurance? Doesn't Dad pay for that?"

"Yeah, but…" Darius looked down at the floor.

"Yeah, but?" I prompted.

Darius started talking fast. "Yeah, but I don't really have a driver's license because I didn't do the shit I needed to do to get it back after my last DUI, and I didn't think I really needed insurance since I didn't really have a license."

"But you drive. You've been driving for like six months."

"Yeah, because I can't take riding my shitty bike like a little kid. So I told everyone I got my license back."

"Where did the car insurance money go?" I asked.

Darius looked at the ceiling. He exhaled hard. "Your food, your clothes, your stupid shampoo and toothpaste. Dad doesn't give us enough! You needed that money to live, okay?"

I started to get really sweaty. My head started spinning from the inside out, like I was swirling down a drain, except I was just sitting there in my bed. "Darius?" I whispered. "What does this mean?"

"It means I'm in deep shit…like a canyon filled with shit, Taco."

"How deep? Like a thousand dollars deep?" I asked.

"I don't know," he said. "Probably deeper. A lot deeper."

Then he turned and disappeared into his basement.

Maggie did come over later. Mary stayed parked out

front. Maggie hugged me and told me she loved me, and she called Darius an idiot before she left. Instead of making me feel better, she just reminded me how everything in the whole world was spinning out of control.

Best day ever?

Best day ever.

You have to keep trying.

CHAPTER 21

Twelve days later after a lot of trouble, which included Darius getting really drunk again and falling down in the yard and puking on the stairs (which I cleaned up) and him missing work due to a massive hangover, Darius got fired from Captain Stabby's.

During that same time, Maggie Corrigan began to show a little more in the baby-belly department. If you didn't know the what-what, you might not be able to tell, but I could. Maggie definitely could tell. Throughout the school day, she'd just burst into tears at the drop of a hat. (Really, if someone dropped their hat on the floor, she would get so sad that she'd cry.) Maggie wouldn't let me hug her or anything. Not even when we were alone in the hallway. When I asked her if she still thought we were in love, she said, "Yes, we're in love. I just hate you right now, but not forever." So I had to guess our plan was still in place.

Here's some more bad news: I had to go to musical practice three times during those couple of weeks, and that meant my nights at Nussbaum's went very late. The musical practices themselves were great though. The other munchkins and I sang our nuts off, and we got our first taste of walking around on our knees to look super tiny, which was hilarious.

The really good news was that I loved being at Nussbaum's. Chatting up the clients? Making coffee and running down to Pancho's for sandwiches? Boom. Good times. I even figured out how Mallory intended to organize the majesty of the law folders and papers, although it was pretty clear that she hadn't been filing squatch since long before she got the babe in her maker.

Dingus, I found unfiled case documents going back like eighteen months. Eighteen months! No lady carries her baby goods for that amount of time. The doctors would come after her with a knife because the baby would have been the size of a full-grown pit bull. Mallory seemed like maybe she was just a sucky worker.

When I figured out that the files were ordered by client's last name and then by month and year—bing bang boom. I filed like a kingpin. It was pretty easy work, but Mr. Nussbaum kept saying what an astonishingly good job I was doing.

After I fulfilled my no-money civic duty, I'd walk home in the cold, feeling like all the world made sense—that is, if you just paid attention, put the right paper in the right folder, and slid it in the right drawer. But then I'd get home and find sad, broken Darius or super drunk Darius like I did one time.

I yelled at him that he was an asshole for drinking again, but he didn't care. He slurred, "I've got no reason for nothing."

Drunk, drunk, drunk.

On the eleventh day, two days after I asked Mr. Nussbaum if Darius needed to hire a lawyer and Mr. Nussbaum laughed and said, "Your brother is so obviously guilty in every facet of his situation. Witnesses and blood tests verify all counts against him. All you'd be doing is adding to the total of this great financial disaster," Darius got the letter from the county clerk telling him what he had to look forward to in the coming year.

Here's the what-what:

1. A $1,100 fine.

2. A twenty-four-month driver's license suspen-
    sion, minimum. (He'd have to do a bunch of
    alcohol assessments and driving courses or it
    would be longer.)

3. A five-week stint (FIVE WEEKS) in the county jail, which would begin on January 2.

4. And then there was the real kick in the salami. He had to pay $22,549.30 in restitution to the local company that franchised the KFC/Taco Bell. That's how much damage my brother did to their drive-through window when he fell asleep and drove his stupid car into the side of the building.

Darius, who was already tender in his man parts, both physical and emotional, fell on the floor, sobbing. I tried to comfort him. He told me to shut up with my sunny crap and go the f-bomb away. So I went back to the master suite. I could still hear him wailing.

Two hours later, he knocked on the door and said, "Taco, I have an alcohol problem. I want to drink right now because I don't know what else to do. I got loaded the other day because I got in a fight with Dad about money. I don't have enough money to buy shoes, and there are holes in mine where the water comes through. But he seriously won't help us anymore."

"Because of Miz?" I asked. "He needs money for her?"

"No, because he's Dad," Darius said. "That's why he won't help. Without Mom, Dad is a bad man."

"Oh," I said.

"I'm a drunk. I don't have money. And I can't make money because I'm going to jail. And that means I can't take care of you the way Mom wanted me to. Things are bad right now. We have to pay rent and utilities and…" Darius's face got all red and splotchy, and his eyes watered. "Man, I hate saying this so much, Taco. I'm such a failure." He looked up at the ceiling. "Please, I'm sorry, Mom, but Taco has to get a job or we're going to all starve and die in the snow." Then he looked back at me. "I'm sorry. I'm sorry. I'm really sorry."

"No," I said. "Don't be sorry. I can handle this." I rolled out of bed. Darius had helped me so much. I could help him and me…and Maggie too. I wasn't scared at all. I was so serious. "I will be a man."

"Oh shit," Darius said. "You have no idea about life."

"I'm totally great with life. I can do this, Darius."

Darius shook his head and closed his eyes. "You're just so full of shit, dude. You kind of make me sick."

"What?" I asked.

Darius deflated. He spoke really quietly. "Seriously. I really don't want to talk to you for a few days, okay? Just stay away from me." He left my room.

I had to tell myself, like, ten thousand times, "Today is the best day I've ever had," because I'll tell you, after that weird display, I had fear in my heart for sure.

When Dad went up north to the mine, it wasn't so he could marry some puffy-coat-wearing lady. It was so he could earn extra money to keep me floating until I was adult enough to float my own boat.

And the reason Darius stopped going to tech school and took a full-time job driving a Pepsi truck and then working full-time at Captain Stabby's was so he could keep me afloat until I could float my own boat.

But Dad floated into Miz's hot sack, and Darius sunk himself all the way to the bottom of the ocean. And Dad wouldn't call me back, and Darius told me to stay away from him. There was no one to float my boat but me, and I didn't even have a boat because, according to Darius, I was full of shit and also I was in high school and I had homework and musical rehearsals and I had to work for Nussbaum for free and… Holy balls, dingus. I had a baby in my girlfriend.

"Today is the best day I've ever had? So is tomorrow?" How could I believe it?

Whatever. I kept repeating it to myself.

"Tomorrow will be even better than today."

And it worked. That night I dreamt that my mom

was watching out for me like a big, bald Tibetan baby-head sun rising over the grocery store.

The next day was my seventeenth birthday.

CHAPTER 22

I t was a Friday, the last day of school before winter break. My birthday!

Not that I cared. My job was to get my shiz together, not get excited about school vacation or birthdays or whatever. But dingus, nobody remembered my birthday. Not Darius (who wouldn't talk to me). Not Dad (who didn't call). Not Maggie Corrigan (who, for reasons that are completely understandable, was wrapped up in her own self). Not Ak Sharma. Not even my oldest pal, Brad Schwartz. Not one single human being.

Except Emily Cook. Sort of.

She caught me in the commons. She was wearing her shirt buttoned all the way up to her collar and her circular plastic nerd glasses. "Hey, Taco! Are you seventeen?" she asked.

I stared at her. I nodded fast. "I am! Today!"

"Oh…sooo…happy birthday?" Emily said.

"Yes! Exactly! It's my birthday," I said. "Thanks for saying happy birthday." I think the word *birthday* sent me into some kind of super awkward info puke because I started talking fast. "When my mom wasn't dead, she used to give me birthday cake first thing in the morning, and *then* we'd go for breakfast at Country Kitchen. Like I needed any *more* food, right?"

"Right?" Emily asked. "Uh…are you okay?"

"I don't know," I said. I took a deep breath. Nobody had talked to me all morning, you know? "Probably not." I shrugged and smiled at Emily. "Hey, why do you care if I'm seventeen? That's pretty weird."

"Oh yeah," Emily said. "One of the college kids who works the desk at the emergency room quit, so we need to hire someone. You have to be seventeen, so I figured I'd ask. I know you're a busy guy, but…"

"Yeah, I really don't have time."

Emily looked down. "I know. Lecroy makes such a big deal out of a musical. It's like he's putting on a real Broadway show, not a rinky-dink high school production."

"That's not it. I need a real job."

Emily shook her head slightly. "Didn't I just mention a job at the hospital?"

"I already volunteer at Nussbaum's law office, so I can't do more charity work."

"What kind of charity work does Nussbaum do? My dad says he's a scoundrel," Emily said.

"Really?" I asked. "Nussbaum?"

"Doesn't he spend all his time gambling at the VFW?" Emily asked.

"Really?"

Emily stared at me a second and then shook out the cobwebs. "Taco, you're kind of an airhead."

"Me?"

"Do you think I work at the emergency room all night long for free?"

"Yeah. Volunteer work. Nerds love that crap, right?"

"I may be a nerd, but I'm not a dolt. I get paid eleven dollars an hour."

I sort of gasped for air. Tibetan sun came flooding in from the commons area skylight. It was a total miracle. "What are you saying, Emily Cook?" I was getting tears in my eyes because I really didn't know how to get a job and here was somebody giving me a shot.

"Uh…you're seventeen, so you should apply for the job at the hospital. That's all."

"Really? I could work at the hospital? For money?" It just seemed so far out of my league, dingus. Such a dream.

"I mentioned you to Dr. Anderson at our staff meeting last night, and he knew your mom really well because they worked together. She was a nurse, right?"

"Yeah! But in Cuba City, not in town."

"He works there too. Anyway, he told me to talk to you because he also heard about how you calmed down that sorority girl when she arrived in the emergency room."

"Yes!" I said. "I am totally at your service! I'll take the job!"

"Well, you have to apply for it first."

"I am a man who can float my own boat," I said.

"Okay. Is that a good thing?" Emily asked. "Can you come into the hospital tomorrow morning?"

"You know it, Emily Cook," I said. "I'll be there."

I walked around the rest of the day with my head held high as a kite floating on helium winds. When the bell rang, I grabbed Maggie Corrigan and said, "I'm going to be a doctor or nurse!"

She said, "Merry Christmas. I'm going to Ohio tonight. It's going to suck."

"I'll miss you, my lady. Safe journeys," I said.

She swallowed like she was about to barf. Then she nodded and left the school. We were definitely working our plan! No one could possibly tell that Maggie liked me at all, much less loved me.

After school, I told Mr. Nussbaum with a no-nonsense voice like it was exactly what had to happen, "I'm going to be late coming to the office tomorrow because I have to go procure employment at Southwest Municipal in the a.m."

Mr. Nussbaum stood up from his desk and pulled on his shirt. He grabbed my hand and walked with me out of his office, through reception, and into the majesty of the law filing room. There, he showed me a pile of new files, which were piled on top of the old files I hadn't yet finished filing. "You still going to have time to pay your debt to society?" Nussbaum asked.

"I will. But I need money."

"Darius?" Mr. Nussbaum asked.

"Yes," I said. "Darius and other stuff."

"Your pops not willing to give you a little extra?" Mr. Nussbaum asked.

"Wouldn't seem so," I said. "He won't take my calls."

"No other way?" he asked.

"I mean, if you paid me for this work, then I wouldn't have to get another job."

"That's not our deal," Mr. Nussbaum said. "I'm already doing my part."

"Okay," I said.

He breathed in and out through his nose and squinted down at me. "Taco. Let's talk about adult problems," he said. He turned and walked back into his office.

He waved that I should follow him, so I did. He sat down in his chair and gestured for me to sit across from him. "It has come to my attention that there are other issues too, aren't there?"

"Beyond Darius and my dad?" I asked.

"Troubles you're not broadcasting to the public," Mr. Nussbaum said.

"What?" I knew what he was talking about, but I didn't think he could possibly know what he was talking about.

"Adult problems related to Maggie Corrigan? Related to her parents? Related to a meeting my friend Bill Bettendorf took earlier today, whereby Maggie's parents want to remove your parental rights over the child she's gestating?"

"Oh shit," I said. "I can't lose my parental rights!"

"Taco. Be real, amigo."

I felt like I was looking up at a giant waterfall that was blasting my face. "Okay. It's all true. Gestating," I said, barely able to get the word out.

"Of course it's true. All of it." Nussbaum nodded at me.

"But, Jesus, can the Corrigans really do that? Remove my rights without me agreeing?"

"If we don't fight them, they can," Mr. Nussbaum said.

"I want to fight! I want to be a dad, a family guy, the husband Maggie needs. I want to kick around a soccer ball with my kid."

Mr. Nussbaum squinted at me again. He kind of laughed. "So you want to get a job *and* work here *and* go to school *and* be a musical munchkin *and* be a dad?"

"Yes," I said.

"Again, you want to be a dad *and* a typical teenager *and* a munchkin?"

"Yes?"

Nussbaum shook his head. He sighed. "I don't think so," he said. "You have to simplify, prioritize, or you're in trouble. You're *already* in trouble."

"Oh," I said. Yeah, dingus, I got it. I just didn't want to get it.

Nussbaum laughed. He barked, "Wow!"

"Wow what?"

He laughed more. "I just can't see how a good kid like you can get into so many messes! That Maggie Corrigan must be one hot tamale. Hard for you to think clearly with her around? Plus you don't have a family to write home about. Not like there's anyone to guide you or clean up your messes. They die or get drunk or run away with floozies up at the mines, don't they?"

"I guess," I said.

"Wow." The smile dropped off Nussbaum's face. He exhaled and stared at me. He didn't say anything for a few seconds, like he was thinking hard. Then he nodded. "Okay, I'm it. I'm your guy, Taco. Listen to me. First things first. Get your priorities straight. You can't quit school to go to work or your future will be ugly. Got it?"

"I won't quit school," I said.

"Good. Also, you can't quit here until Mallory gets back or you're in trouble with the law," Nussbaum said.

"Okay." I wouldn't quit.

He leaned back, put his hands behind his head, and kept thinking and talking. "You need money. Your dad won't support you the way you need to be supported."

"True," I said.

"Well, we could sue the shit out of him. You're his responsibility."

"No!" I shouted.

"But your brother is going to jail, and you need money," Nussbaum said. "Why not get it from your old man?"

"I don't want to be connected to him…like indebted," I explained.

"But you need money," Nussbaum said.

"So?"

"So you won't become homeless. So you won't starve."

"Also, so Maggie and my baby have food to eat when they come live in the house with me."

Nussbaum shook his head. Then he looked up and spoke to the ceiling, "But you're just a kid."

"I'm not really a kid. I'm seventeen today," I said.

"Yeah, yeah," Mr. Nussbaum said. "But you don't need to have a kid."

"What does that mean?" I asked. "I'm the father of a baby."

Nussbaum leaned forward. "Taco. You forget that crap, amigo. Take a sizable cash settlement from the Corrigan family, give up your parental rights and all nonessential contact with Maggie, and go be a teen and a musical munchkin who lives in your own place and has enough to eat."

"No!" I shouted. There it was! What Maggie said they were going to do! They wanted me to sell my kid! "I won't do that."

"You haven't even heard their offer, Taco."

"I don't sell children. I don't sell my love."

"Oh boy," Nussbaum said. "Will you just hear their offer?"

I clapped my hands over my ears. "No, no, no, no!"

Mr. Nussbaum shouted, "Stop it! Stop, Taco!"

I put my hands down, glared at Nussbaum, and said,

"So other than sell children for money, what do you think I should do?"

"Go get a job. That's all you can do," he said. "Then between here, school, and your job, work yourself to death."

"Okay," I said. "I'm on it."

Nussbaum glared at me. "Cut the deluded shit. You quit that musical because you have no time to be a damn munchkin. Focus, kid. You have school, my office, and whatever job you get, and that's it. You agree to quit that musical and dedicate yourself, and I'll fight off the Corrigans. Do we have a deal?"

"Yes, sir," I said quietly. I needed help. "Thank you."

Mr. Nussbaum just shook his head.

A few minutes later, I was back filing. My stomach hurt, and my chin trembled. For my birthday I got the gift of no longer being Mayor of Munchkinland.

I got Nussbaum's help though. That meant something.

CHAPTER 23

Here's the deal. I have sometimes thought Danielle Corrigan was a mean witch and not a great mom (although I can see her point of view with regard to me). At the same time, I have always thought Reggie Corrigan was a righteous fellow.

Thus, when Maggie told me that her parents wanted to pay me off, I figured it was all Danielle Corrigan's doing. I imagined Danielle going through her purse, digging out a twenty, and saying in her very mean voice, "That scrungy little dirt ball can't even afford protein. Let's give him a twenty in return for his disappearance from our lives!" I figured Maggie overheard that conversation and got really mad and told me about it as part of her ploy to stop her mother's evil ways.

I also figured that Reggie's clear and kind head would prevail. "We cannot purchase the fool's rights, darling. Rights are unassailable. They're intrinsic to being human."

But if their lawyer was telling my Nussbaum that the Corrigans wanted to buy my rights, Reggie had to be onboard too. That was another kick in the salad, another blow to my *best day ever* philosophy of life.

But no. Hell no. The Corrigans couldn't buy anything from me. No way! I wouldn't sell them the shirt off my back, not for a million dollars, not even if they were naked in the snow. I wanted nothing more to do with the Corrigans.

I needed money though, and that meant—per my conversation with Nussbaum—I had to do something about the musical. It weighed on me. It ruined my good times.

That night Brad Schwartz (who remembered my birthday at the end of the day) picked me up from Nussbaum's. Sharma met us over at Brad's house, and his mom gave us each a cupcake. (Mine had a candle in it.) They sang "Happy Birthday," and then Brad and Sharma played chess for a couple hours while I watched and ate 116 Geno's pizza rolls (maybe not quite that many, but close).

"Come on. You don't want in on this game, birthday boy?" Sharma asked at one point.

"Oh. No, my brother," I said.

He just shrugged.

Even if I wanted to play chess, I couldn't. I had all that munchkin weight on my mind. Mr. Lecroy. Witches, scarecrows, Dorothy, and flying monkeys.

Before midnight, Brad drove me home. On the way he said, "You have anyplace to go for Christmas?"

"No," I said. "Maybe my dad will come down, but I don't want to hang with him, so no, I've got no plans."

"Now you do," Brad said. "Mom asked me to ask you to come over Christmas Eve and to stay overnight. We'll eat cookies. Watch *Elf* and *A Christmas Story*. Sound good?"

"Very, very, very good," I said.

"You hang tough, man," Brad said when I got out of the car.

The Schwartz family? They're good people, dingus. But no, I couldn't enjoy them.

All evening, I'd been thinking about Nussbaum saying, "Cut the deluded shit." Musical munchkins and the life of the typical American teenager were no longer within reach for this guy.

When I got inside the house, Darius was either asleep or dead. (His shoes were at the top of the stairs, so I knew he couldn't be out.) That he wasn't drunk and disorderly certainly was good. I looked in the fridge because I was still hungry even after I had downed all those pizza rolls. The refrigerator was totally and completely empty, pal.

Then I sat down at the table, cranked up the old computer, and sent Mr. Lecroy the following message:

206

Dear Sir,

It has come to my attention that I no longer
have enough money to stay alive. Thus, I am
sad to say that I will be backing out of my
role as Mayor of Munchkinland. I am resign-
ing from all responsibilities associated with
this year's production of *The Wizard of Oz*,
which is certain to be magnificent. I do so
with a heavy heart but also with an iron will
to stand my ground and be the best Taco I
can be. Thank you for your support. I look
forward to cheering wildly at the curtain call
of the final performance.

Sincerely,
William (Taco) Keller

Mr. Lecroy was apparently awake at one in the
morning. He responded immediately from his iPhone.

Taco! Noooo! There must be other means of
assistance? We need you.

I sat back, took in a deep breath, and said out loud,

"My problems are real. This is real." Then I typed back to Mr. Lecroy:

Dear Sir,

It is time for me to take my responsibilities seriously. At times like these, the musical, although the greatest joy of my life (outside of making out with Maggie Corrigan), must take a backseat to providing for myself and my family.

Thank you,
William Keller

I shut down the computer so I wouldn't get into a long email conversation with Mr. Lecroy. Facts are facts. I didn't want to explain the facts. Then I worried about writing that thing about making out with Maggie Corrigan. *Why do you say such shit all the time?*

"You're so dumb!" I shouted at myself.

"Shut up!" Darius shouted from the basement.

I guess I was happy he wasn't dead.

CHAPTER 24

The next morning, the first morning of winter break, I entered the same hospital door I'd gone through when Darius had passed out and hit the Taco Bell. There, sitting behind her reception desk, was Emily Cook.

"Hi!" she said. "You've got a meeting with my manager in twenty minutes, okay? Dr. Anderson already mentioned you to her, so that's good. Fill out this application." She handed me a one-page app.

"Got a pen?" I asked her.

Five minutes later, I'd filled out the form. It was pretty cool because I already had some job experience. I listed Brad's dad as a reference for the pool. And better yet, the application asked me to explain any experience I might have had at filing and running a reception desk. Well, I had several weeks of hard-core filing and receiving under my belt from working for Nussbaum!

Seemed to me the job was in the hole, dingus.

But Emily's boss, Ms. Poller, wasn't so sure.

Her office was totally hot—like sweaty, not sexy. So

I felt a little dizzy and wasn't at the top of my game. The first thing she said was this: "I live two doors down from Danielle and Reggie Corrigan. You're the kid who keeps climbing their house, aren't you?"

Well, how was I supposed to answer that? Should I have said no? Not me? I'm not the guy when clearly I'm the Taco who climbs houses in her neighborhood? I said, "Yeah, I'm Maggie's…" I almost said boyfriend, but we were pretending not to be in love, so I caught myself. "We're pals. She's their daughter."

"I know," Ms. Poller said. "I've known Maggie since she was a little girl."

I sweated really badly right then. I might've spritzed Ms. Poller because the perspiration just shot out of me, but I got myself under control. "I'm not climbing their house anymore. Last time I did, the Corrigans weren't home, and I set off an alarm. I was almost charged with criminal trespassing! It's lucky the cops know I'm a good kid."

"You were injured the time before, if I remember correctly," Ms. Poller said.

"Growing up is hard to do," I said. "But I've learned my lesson well."

Ms. Poller smiled at that, and I was very relieved, dingus.

She reviewed my application while I worried if she'd think my handwriting was neat enough and I had the experience necessary. Then she said, "This job is twenty hours a week, sometimes more. Do you have time? You'll be working two overnight shifts and a half-shift on the weekend."

I thought about the twenty hours I was putting in at Nussbaum's and calc, but I also thought about Darius and Dad and my baby and Maggie's large appetite and need for hair dryers, shower additions, and clean towels when she moves in, so I said, "I am prepared to take as many hours as you'll give me."

Ms. Poller nodded. "Dr. Anderson told me about your people skills—how you helped with that young patient when you were here to visit your brother."

"Yes," I said as nobly as I could, although all I'd done was be myself with that girl.

"I'm a little reticent due to your history of climbing houses. But that's done, right? No more odd behavior?" she asked.

"Absolutely. Done and done."

"I really enjoyed the few times I met your mother," she said.

"She was a good person," I said.

Ms. Poller nodded. A smile flashed on her lips, and

her eyes seemed to water a little. She picked up my application again. "Oh, Bill Nussbaum is our lawyer," she said. "He'll give you a good reference? Barry Schwartz too?"

"Those guys think I'm the cat's meow," I said. What the hell does that even mean? Cat's meow? It just came out.

Ms. Poller smiled wide. "I bet we'll agree with them. We don't usually move so quickly, but we are short-staffed…you're hired, Mr. Keller. Emily will start training you tomorrow."

I didn't tell her not to call me Mr. Keller. I didn't jump out of my chair and give her a fist bump. I didn't plant a wet kiss on her mouth. I simply reached over the desk and shook her hand because at that moment, I was proud to be Mr. Keller, a man with a job and the demeanor to match.

CHAPTER 25

The work at the hospital was not hard.

Emily trained me in, like, ten minutes. Pretty much all I did was sit at that reception desk and stare at the door, where almost nobody ever entered. My schedule was 11:00 p.m. on Monday night to 7:30 a.m. on Tuesday morning, same thing on Thursday nights (to Friday mornings), and eight to midnight on Sundays. Emily said that pretty much the only consistently crazy times in the ER were Friday and Saturday nights during the college semester when kids were drunk, although occasionally whacky things would go down on Thursday.

The fact that it wasn't hard didn't make it exactly easy though.

Still, for a full twenty-four hours, I believed that balancing Nussbaum law, hospital work, and school would be a piece of cake.

It started with my first shift, the Sunday shift, which was fine because nothing happened. It wasn't that late at night, and I got to chat up the nurses, who told a lot of dirty jokes. Because it was break, I didn't have school on Monday. That was good because I didn't wake up until eleven. I spent the afternoon at Nussbaum's. He had a client arrive at four fifteen, so I made coffee, greeted her, and shot the shit. ("Hiya, how you doing today, Mrs. Walters? Oh yeah, you'll get your money back with Nussbaum on your side!") I filled out a couple forms, and I hit filing from four thirty to about five. Then Nussbaum asked me to run to Pancho's for some sammies. Got back about 5:20. Nussbaum and I ate, and he asked me a bunch of questions like, "If you stop short because a dog runs in front of your car and the car behind you hits you, are you at fault for the accident? You were the one to apply sudden brakeage, correct?"

The answer to that puzzle, in case you were wondering, is no. The car behind you was following too closely if they didn't have time to stop when you stopped. It is *their* fault, not your fault. Seems to me old Nussbaum could've been teaching me some more complex shiz, but whatever.

I also cleaned the bathroom and vacuumed the reception area. By that time it was 7:15 p.m. Nussbaum headed to the VFW for cards, and I hoofed it on home. I tried to go straight to sleep because I knew I wouldn't have another chance to catch sweet slumber before morning, but I couldn't go to sleep because this Taco couldn't ever find slumber earlier than about 11:00 p.m.

And at 11:00 p.m., I began to see how difficult my new responsible life would be.

I was sitting behind the desk at the hospital when I started to get tired, but I couldn't go to sleep because I was getting paid to watch the door. So I tried to study calc to stay awake, but my eyes were all bleary. My head swam, and my muscles started to give out. I drank some hot chocolate with a bunch of bad coffee in it, which helped. At about 2:15 a.m., right as I thought couldn't take it anymore, the phone rang. The ambulance guy said they were coming in with two dudes who had gotten into a knife fight behind a bar on Second Street. Neither of the guys had stab wounds, but they had both slipped on ice and gotten their hands all cut up on broken glass.

It was intense! I was filled with adrenaline as I prepped the nurses and orderlies with the news. When the ambulance arrived, the two guys were covered in blood, and one guy had actually stabbed himself when he fell down. There was a lot of excitement and shouting, and then one dude's elderly mom showed up and tried to hit the guy her son had been fighting. She swung her purse at him! An orderly had to restrain her, and I was able to talk her down. Turns out she knew my dead grandma. It was total mayhem for like two hours!

I was all razzed up for the rest of my shift until my replacement showed up at seven. I told the replacement all about what had happened, but I had forgotten to scan and file the two guys' paperwork. She said, "Thank God! I have something to do." I was glad that made her feel useful.

I hoofed it home through a snowstorm and crashed on the couch. *In two weeks you'll be in school after your shift*, I thought. At least I had Christmas break to relax and get acclimated, right?

Except it wasn't relaxing at all. The next day the Corrigans, even though they'd left town for the holidays, deposited a Christmas-sized load of pain in my mailbox in the form of an official petition to release me from my parental rights, which, according to the memo from their dick lawyer, I was supposed to sign…or else.

Or else? I sure as hell wasn't going to sign it!

I carried it over to Nussbaum's office. He already had a copy.

The problem was, as Nussbaum told me, being seventeen and not eighteen meant that my dad could, in fact, sign the paperwork for me without my consent and that his signature would be legally binding. My dad, who didn't want me around anymore, surely wouldn't want a grandkid to go with the two sons he already didn't like.

How was I going to hide this from Dad for months and months?

I needed to know if Dad got a copy of the petition. Nussbaum said we couldn't just ask the Corrigans' lawyer because that would tip him off that he should send a petition directly to Dad if he hadn't already. "Bettendorf isn't the brightest bulb, amigo, but he did get through law school," Nussbaum told me. I called Dad like ten times until he finally picked up.

"What?" he asked instead of saying hi.

"So how are things going?" I asked. "You and Miz having some nice nights out on the town? Get any strange voice mails from lawyers or whatnot?"

"What are you getting at, Taco?" Dad asked.

I used Darius as an excuse. "Well, you know, Darius has to go to jail on January 2, but I haven't gotten any official correspondence, so I was just wondering."

"Me and Darius have talked. I'm driving him to Lancaster on the second. Already took off work."

"Will you be here for Christmas?"

"Can't do that. See you on New Year's," Dad said.

"So you haven't gotten any official mail at all?" I asked.

"No. Why would I? Darius is an adult."

So that was good. The Corrigans hadn't contacted Dad.

Nussbaum had his own copy of the petition, and I decided to cut mine into a bunch of little pieces and toss it in the trash.

It was a symbolic gesture. Nussbaum said that the petition was a first step, not the last, and the Corrigans would be coming after my parental rights through the courts soon enough. "You should take the money from them now," he said. "Even with me advocating for you, I can't guarantee they won't get what they're after. Take the money they're offering, amigo," Nussbaum told me.

"That's not how I roll."

Nussbaum shook his head. "Why don't you at least ask how much money they'll give you?"

"Haven't you asked?"

"They haven't given me a number yet, but yes, I'm going to find out," Nussbaum said.

"Don't tell me," I said.

Nussbaum sighed like a drama queen. "Listen, amigo. I've been thinking a lot about this. You have quite a few strikes against you. You're broke. You've been in trouble with the police. Your brother has also been drunk and disorderly. One way or another, the Corrigans are going to get your butt in a sling. Please. Listen. You might as well be compensated for your pain."

Nussbaum wasn't listening to me. "That is not how I roll!" I shouted.

Nussbaum gestured for me to leave his office.

If no one was going to fight for me, I was going to fight for myself. On Friday morning, instead of going home after my shift at the hospital, I slogged through ice and snow to Nussbaum's. His Internet was superfast, and he let me use his laptop. I did research while he spent most of the day, which was Christmas Eve, at the VFW.

According to the Internet, I had to prove my fitness as a parent if a judge was going to let me keep my rights. Through research I found out that other fathers in my position had protected their rights by sending their pregnant mamas weekly checks, by writing weekly correspondence to check up on the health of their fetus, and by taking birthing and parenting classes. If you had documentation for all that, you could put up a good fight.

I called Nussbaum's cell to ask him a couple questions. He answered, "Mallory? What the hell?"

"No. Taco," I said.

"Oh yeah. I got the office phone plugged in as Mallory," Nussbaum said. He was slurring his words like Darius.

GEOFF HERBACH

"If I send Maggie Corrigan money to show I'm covering baby expenses, do I need to open a checking account? I could, like, photocopy the cash, but that doesn't seem like very good proof that I'm actually sending the money," I said.

"Oh, Taco," Nussbaum said. "What money you gonna send? Who's money, kid?"

"Mine."

"You gonna not eat so you can send her money?"

"If that's what it takes."

He sighed. "Checking account," he said. "You bet."

"Okay. One other thing. Does my health class at school count as a parenting class if I'm trying to prove I've gotten parenting training?"

"What do you do in your class?" he asked.

"One time we had to carry an egg around for a week and take care of it so we could see how hard it is to take care of a baby. I smashed mine because I tripped on my pants."

Nussbaum laughed really loud.

"It's not funny. Does that count?"

"No. You need a real class up at the clinic. You learn about birth and the proper way to bathe a baby. Swaddle its little butt. That kind of thing."

"Really? At the hospital? Like, where I work?"

"What the hell other hospital would I be talking about for Christ's sake?"

220

"I gotta go," I said and hung up.

I'll tell you what, dingus, that Nussbaum knows his business.

I spent Christmas with the Schwartz family, which was warm and fun. Mrs. Schwartz baked a million cookies and wore a hilarious reindeer sweater and a Santa hat. But it also made me feel like shit because Darius was home alone.

During my next hospital shift over break, I wandered back into the nursery and found a pamphlet about these birth classes that they hold every other week on Wednesday nights. The next course started in January. By March, Maggie and I—if I could get her to attend with me because these suckers were clearly geared to couples expecting first babies, not just the dads—could get totally stamped and certified as adult-sized baby makers with mad delivery skills. That would look good to a judge.

Maggie hadn't been responding to my emails, but when I got home from work, I sent her the particulars of the class anyway. I said it was an absolute must that we attend to learn how to get the baby out of her in a healthy way. I said that it was of utmost importance that she respond to my email so I could reserve our position in the class. Then I went to sleep.

By ten the next morning, she hadn't replied.

I took a nap and checked my email, but there was still no reply. Had her parents taken away her smartphone? Maybe she didn't have access to her iPad or a computer, so she couldn't respond.

I went to Nussbaum's and did more filing.

During a break, I checked my email on Nussbaum's computer, but Maggie hadn't replied.

Then I started to feel heavy in my heart and tired and sad about the whole Maggie thing, like maybe she just wanted to be done with me, wanted me to let go of my parental rights and disappear. So I wrote to her again and didn't mention the baby, just said,

I love you. Hope you had a beautiful Christmas with your family.

I sat at Nussbaum's desk with my head in my hands for maybe five minutes. When I looked up, Maggie had responded!

I love you. Sorry about everything. It's hell on wheels here. Everything is hell on wheels, man. Merry Christmas. I'm with you in my dreams.

Yes! The thing was still *on*!

222

The thing being our love, I guess, and our plan too.

That night at the hospital, Emily Cook hung out with me, even though I was the only one getting paid. I guess she didn't have anything better to do. It wasn't busy because the college kids were all home for winter break, so she told me a bunch of stuff about her that I didn't know. In fact, I didn't know anything about her except that she played the cello really well.

She's a total loner. Her best friend, Andrew Reinstein, moved away after eighth grade. I kind of remember him. He was a nerd, but he was pretty funny. What's weird is that his brother was this super-stud jock who won state in track and played football with Cody Frederick. The dude went to Stanford for football.

But Andrew moved to Florida, and Emily was super lonely. She became friends with this very weird dude, Curtis Bode's brother. (Curtis shot himself in eighth grade. Man, that was the worst, and it was right when my mom got diagnosed too.) As weird as Curtis Bode's brother was, he was a great artist. Emily wrote stories and he drew them, so they made these rad comic books. But then he moved to Stitzer, which was too bad. That kid was so poor, he didn't even have email or anything. He was totally gone after he left town, so Emily had spent the last couple years basically friendless, other than her cello.

"Right now you're the only person in school I talk to…ever," Emily said.

"Nobody?"

"Seriously. I can go whole weeks without even uttering a noise at school. I don't even talk to teachers."

"That is crazy! You're awesome," I told her. "You should talk."

"No."

"I talk to everyone."

"I know," she said. "I don't understand how you can like people so much."

"People are the best," I said. "They're funny and great. Curtis Bode's brother isn't the only one who can draw, you know? Andrew Reinstein isn't the only nerd on the block. There are basketfuls of nerds drawing great pictures right now as we speak. You gotta meet them! You gotta talk so you can meet all those weirdos!"

Emily's eyes got watery. She smiled that giant smile of hers. "Maybe I'll try a little harder," she said. "Or maybe I'll wait until college."

"Do whatever you feel in your heart," I said.

"You mean that un-ironically, don't you?"

"What do you mean?" I asked.

"You just made my point," she said.

"Good," I said. "Glad to be of service."

Before she left, Emily Cook kissed me on the cheek. It seemed like a sister kind of kiss, so I enjoyed it. She didn't show up during my Thursday night shift, which bummed me out.

On the day before New Year's (people call that New Year's Eve), I got my first paycheck and opened a checking account. The lady at Mound City Bank told me I had a savings account too, which I knew because it was my swimming pool money, but I asked her to keep this new account separate out of respect for Darius's wish that I use that pool money for college. I try to be a good brother to him, and honestly whatever swimming pool money was in there wasn't nearly enough to help us anyway. Then with a little cash I kept out (I got paid like $330 total, which seemed like so much!), I ordered pizza from Steve's. Darius and I ate like kings. We watched all the Jason Bourne movies. Darius, who was in a pretty fine mood considering everything, jumped up and started kicking and punching the air in the middle of one of the movies and said he thought he could probably be like Jason Bourne if he joined the military. This was the kind of crap he'd say to me when we were little kids back at the mullet house. It was fun to see him so jacked up.

The next day Dad showed up. He and Darius went to his hotel, and they had a bunch of drinks. Dad didn't invite me to go with them, but before they left, he asked if I'd taken care of the baby situation.

"Yup," I said. "Doing it."

"Doing what?" he asked.

"Taking care of it," I said.

"Good. You'd better...or else."

"Or else?" I asked. "Why does everybody say or else?"

"Because they all want to kick your ass," Dad said. "They're just looking for the right excuse." Then he said, "I checked with Nussbaum, and legally you can live here by yourself since you're seventeen, so don't worry about that while Darius is away."

"I know," I said. "I checked already."

Dad looked at me for a moment. "Good," he said. Then Dad was gone.

Darius went to jail the next day. We said good-bye while Dad waited in the car. I told him I'd come up and visit. He told me not to. Then I slept all day. Then I worked. Then I slept.

Then it was the end of Christmas break. Not a bad break, all things considered.

CHAPTER 26

M aggie Corrigan showed up at my house before school on Tuesday, our first day back. I'd gotten off work at the hospital a few minutes early and had just arrived at the house myself. Maggie rang the bell and then entered without me opening the door. (I was in the bathroom reapplying deodorant when the bell rang.)

I met her in the living room. She wore the biggest Christmas sweater in the whole world and a scarf and a hat. She looked like some kind of bundled Santa elf who was probably pregnant but maybe just really thick and powerful through her midsection.

"Holy shit! What are you doing here?" I was so happy to see her, dingus.

"I had Mary drop me off for school at seven. I told her that I had a cheerleading meeting, but I lied. I had to see you. I thought about you the whole break."

"Me too. I mean, I thought about a lot of stuff, including you," I said.

"Oh?" Maggie's face grew sad.

"All the good stuff was about you, all the productive and good… Wait. Wait here. I have to get something."

"Okay," Maggie said. She still looked sad.

I ran back into my room to get the envelope.

I'd spent the better part of a Christmas break morning crafting a letter of highest quality that I meant to give to Maggie at school, but with her standing right there, I couldn't wait to hand it off. She opened it and read it.

January 3
To: Ms. Maggie Corrigan
From: Mr. William (Taco) Keller

Dear Lady,

I write this letter to make it fully known how much I adore you. When I see you cheer or dance, I am likely to fall over because your excellence and energy are the perfect complement to my own. There are many things I love about you—your sense of humor, that you call me "man" when you're talking to me, your sheer speed when running, your righteous anger when placed in untenable situations, your knees (they look great), your eyes that communicate both love and hate like laser guns, your tenderness when I got hurt and my brother was arrested, your steadfast dedication to our love in the face of resistance from your parents. What could they know of our love? They are not part of this thing between us. And now that you're having our baby, I will love that kid with the same fierce loyalty I have for you. I will climb cliffs and dive into shark-infested oceans to show that kid I'm its dad for life. Because of my own home troubles, I value family more than most. I hope you are feeling well, and I hope you've been making regular doctor visits. And I can't wait until the baby is born so we can live like the family we already are in my heart. I have enclosed a check for $50 and will give you $50 every two weeks to help you take care of any hair- body- or spiritual-related expenses that you might have. I do this because I am yours and you are mine.

Love always,
William (Taco) Keller

Maggie read the letter, and she got really teary. She grabbed my ears with her hands and pulled my face into hers. She said, "I want to take you out for pizza with this check. That's a spiritual-related expense, man, okay?"

"How about you and me get some pizza before we go to our first baby class next week?"

Maggie sighed. "I read your email. But do we really need to do that? My plan is to take a billion drugs and try not to remember I'm having a baby when the time comes."

"No, we have to do it for…for ourselves. They'll teach us how to clean and feed and take care of our baby. I don't know how to do that." I didn't tell Maggie that I was also insisting we go to this class because it would keep us out of legal hot sauce with her parents. Maggie didn't need that kind of stress while in her delicate state, dingus. That's what I told myself.

"Okay," Maggie said. "I'm in. I'll do this for you, okay? We're going to do this thing right."

"Thanks, baby," I whispered.

It was like old times, except new, dingus. We walked to school, holding hands through our mittens, showing our love to the whole world. It was super icy out, so we did some running and skeetch sliding on our shoes. Maggie Corrigan is one of the best shoe skiers I've ever seen. She slid all the way down the hill on Kase Street, probably like two hundred yards, and she was going easily forty or fifty miles per hour. By the time we got to school, we were in the best mood ever. We were having the time of our lives being who we were—Taco and Maggie, the best couple in the state of Wisconsin. We were riding the Good Times Express, a fantastic, luxury love train.

When we entered the commons, everybody stared at us. Everybody looked at Maggie's giant reindeer sweater, which may or may not have been hiding the fact she's pregnant. But who cared? "Let's be pregnant," I whispered.

"We are," Maggie said. "But don't tell anyone."

"Okay," I said. "Let them figure it out for themselves."

"Yeah," she said.

That day was awesome. Mags and I walked the halls, heads held high. People acted weird toward us. Like they were confused why we were back together. We walked hand in hand and made out between classes just like we had last spring and during the fall. But nobody shouted, "Get a room!" or, "More tongue!" like they used to. Instead they all stared at us, at that giant Santa reindeer sweater, which Maggie wore every day that week.

You know, in many ways it was a great week. There was a basketball game Tuesday night, and I played the bass drum in the pep band like I was a mountain gorilla on a bender. Due to my shift at the emergency room, I hadn't had more than a ten-minute nap in, like, thirty-four hours, so I sort of was that gorilla. Maggie cheered in a sweater that stretched across her belly. We didn't really talk at the game because we didn't want adults to see us in action. Teachers saw us together during school, but whatever.

On Wednesday after I slept like a zombie, Maggie and I made out in the school foyer by the auto shop. Her belly pressed against me. It hadn't before, so it was sort of weird. And I worked like a madman at Nussbaum's that night because there was a lot of new filing. I worked so hard that I passed out on the floor of his office and only woke up at 3:00 a.m. Then I walked home, terrified through the ghost hour and feverish cold.

On Thursday, I slept in calc and in English, and Maggie and I made out while people stared at us. Our plan was working great! Except Emily Cook wouldn't talk to me, and Mr. Lecroy pulled me into the choir office on Friday afternoon and begged me to come back to the musical.

"The munchkins are just so uninspired," he said. "Please. All is forgiven. We just need you back."

I walked out without saying a word because I wasn't sure if I was dreaming. Just like I wasn't sure if Mr.

Edwards had screamed at me in calc or not, but probably he had.

All I knew was that Maggie and I were back together and that we were going for it. And wasn't that great? Wasn't that perfect? I'd written her a letter. I'd given her a check. I was being a man. So what if I was super dizzy and I fell down in the hall twice because my leg muscles were tired? Still…weren't these the greatest days ever?

That's what I thought, although I was very tired.

CHAPTER 27

Maggie gave Mary the same excuse so she could come over before school on Monday the next week, but that was all that was the same. Everything else was different. Maggie didn't look at all happy in her peppy Santa reindeer sweater.

I wasn't the same either. I was in my underpants under my covers when she showed up. I wanted to stay in bed for the rest of my life.

The weekend had been totally exhausting.

First Nussbaum and I had worked all day Saturday because he had a big accident case going to court in Lancaster the following week. He got me reading law books and photocopying cases and highlighting important parts of the decisions, which was sort of fun, but it took a lot of concentration.

Secondly, on Saturday night, Sharma came over, and we did calc for three hours. Sounds fantastic, right? Not so fantastic because Sharma was sad. He said, "Remember when we used to watch movies and drive around town with Brad? We'd go eat subs up on the Big M?"

"Yeah. Good times," I said. "Very good times."

"Or remember when your mom made each of us our own pizza and we had a Ping-Pong tournament that lasted all night?" Sharma asked.

"That was three years ago this spring, right? We sure had fun, man, even though Darius smashed our Ping-Pong balls at the end," I said.

"Now all we do is your homework when we hang out. It's not that fun."

"It's pretty fun," I said, trying to sound as if today was the best day ever.

"Not really," Sharma said.

On Sunday, I met Nussbaum at 9:30 a.m. for a doughnut at the Piggly Wiggly. I walked there in the snow because Nussbaum said he couldn't pick me up. We worked until 5:00 p.m.

I tried to do homework after work. (Nussbaum—that sweet man—decided he could drive me home after we got done with our lawyering.) But nothing Sharma had showed me the night before made sense anymore. It was like Sharma's calc lessons hadn't sunk into my brain at all.

Then I did my Sunday shift at the hospital. But

what should've been a good time to read *Romeo and Juliet* for Mrs. Mullen turned into blood central. Four middle school kids went sledding over at the golf course—in the damn dark! And they smacked into a big oak tree. They were screaming and broken, and their parents were freaking out. Dr. Steidinger and Dr. Anderson both had to come down to the ER because we had two wicked concussions, a broken forearm, and one girl with a fat lip from hitting her teeth into the back of another kid's head.

Anyway, I ended up playing with all these little brothers and sisters in the reception area until, like, 1:00 a.m., which was fun, except when they all got super tired. This four-year-old girl fell asleep on my lap, and she put her little hand on my chest. Her wrist was so tiny, and her forehead was so small. She really looked breakable, which scared me. I got super sweaty and itchy, and the itching wouldn't stop, so I couldn't really sleep when I got home.

By the next morning when Maggie showed in her Santa reindeer sweater, I was so wiped out, so dead to the world, dingus, I would have slept through the day. So it was good she showed up because I had to go to school. There was a major test in calc (not that I could remember how to do any calc).

I had no Taco sauce to give, but Maggie needed my

sauce. She sat down on my bed as I blinked awake, and she said, "My mom is a total succubus."

"A succubus?" I mumbled. "Isn't that a supernatural sex demon?"

"Well, she's not that, but she sucks, okay?"

"I'm sorry," I said, trying to be more awake. "Moms are the greatest people in the world, but they can suck when they're not on their 'A' games."

"She's never been on her 'A' game," Maggie whispered. She lay back next to me, her pregnancy bump this weird hill in front of us. "She was hating on me all weekend, as if this baby thing was new news. She just kept staring at the bump and telling me I did this to myself."

"Wow. She really sucks," I said.

"Yeah, and I have really bad acid reflux, man. Mom told me I deserve it because I ate myself sick."

"That's not polite. You don't eat too much," I said.

Maggie sat up and stared at me. "She meant you. She said acid reflex is what I get for eating Taco. She said that nobody's dumb enough to eat Taco and think they're not going to get sick."

"You didn't eat me," I said. Her mom confused me so much.

"She said I'm as stupid as a Taco," Maggie said.

"Jesus," I said. I was starting to fall apart. I couldn't

take it. "I'm not stupid. What the hell? I'm really not. I'm smart, and I'm nice and try really hard all the damn time! Can't she see that? Is your mom blind? Is she just a hate-filled witch who can only see awful shit?"

"I don't know," Maggie said. "I don't think she's right about you or anything."

"Are you sure?" I asked.

"I think so. I don't know! I feel so sick!"

And then both Maggie and I started crying. I don't know exactly why Maggie was crying. But I was so tired, and I missed my mom, who told me how great I was. And I was mad that Maggie's mom hurt my feelings so much. I always liked being a Taco before I met Maggie and her mom. I loved me.

On the way to school, we didn't do any skeetching, but Maggie slipped backward and hit her butt on the ice. I picked her up and carried her for about ten feet until I slipped. She fell on top of me, and we both lay out there on Kase Street on the ice and cried.

Then we started laughing because it was pretty funny too.

"It's like we're both having strokes, man," Maggie said.

"Yeah. Like when Darius took one of mom's Vicodins and a bunch of NyQuil. He fell down the stairs because his body didn't work." We both laughed and did our best to climb back on the Good Times Express. "We're going to be okay, okay?" I whispered to her.

Maggie nodded. She kissed me. "Okay."

Except the tracks for the Good Times Express stopped at school. Everybody stared at Maggie and the rising cake in her oven. It was as if they all got the memo at the same time.

Pss pss pss pss.

"Taco," Maggie said. "They're all whispering about me."

Pss pss pss.

"Nah," I said.

"I'm not ready," Maggie said.

"It's okay. We can't keep it a secret. They're all going to see at some point, you know?"

Maggie started crying again and took off running like a pregnant gazelle. I ran like a dad gazelle after her, but even still, I couldn't keep up with the girl. She shot straight into the girls' bathroom. I started to go in, but Ms. Tindall, who was standing outside her classroom across the hall, was all like, "Taco! You go in and you die."

I stopped in my tracks, exhaled hard, and said, "I know. You're right."

"You'd better believe I'm right," Ms. Tindall said.

Two minutes later the bell rang. I shouted at the door, "See you in English, okay, Maggie?"

She didn't reply.

Maggie did show up to English. When she walked in, I saw what everybody else saw. Her belly was popped up, not down like when somebody gains weight. It was as baby as baby gets. Mrs. Mullen cocked and mouthed, "Whoa."

Maggie smiled. "Surprise! I'm pregnant! Take all in!" She posed and smiled. Then she took the seat right next to me.

"We're going to be okay," she whispered. "We're going to be okay, okay?"

"You're damn straight we're going to be okay," I whispered back. "I have no worries whatsoever."

Mrs. Mullen started class like five minutes late because she couldn't seem to get her words out and she had to go to the bathroom. While she was gone, the whole class turned to stare at me and Maggie. Their mouths hung open, and their eyes watered like they were monkey zombies. Nobody said anything, except Maggie, who started turning red in the face. She said, "Hey, dick bags! Mind your own business!"

The rest of the day went just like that too. It was Maggie and me against the whole openmouthed, whispering school. They didn't seem like they were going to attack us *Lord of the Flies* style, yet they couldn't take their eyes off us either. "We're going to be okay," I said to Maggie at lunch.

"Yeah!" she shouted really loud. She smiled too hard, dingus. Scary smile.

After school, she acted like a total spazmo.

"We're going to be just great! Awesome! Killer awesome!" Maggie said when the last bell rang. She kissed me. She high-fived me. And she went out the door to meet Mary, who was picking her up.

You know, pal, even with her spazmo flying full sail, I tried to believe her, tried to keep riding on the Good Times Express, but later when I was at Nussbaum's, I had a hard time concentrating on the majesty of the law files.

Spazmo. Spazmo. Spazmo.

I took over for Emily Cook at the emergency desk at eight. She didn't look at me or talk to me, even though I was all like, "Hi! What's happening?"

She walked straight out the door. I chased her. "Seriously. Emily, what's happening?"

But she didn't answer.

And then I had to sit there for hours filled with my enormous worry, which totally kicked my energy sack. It took me, like, an hour to walk home in the morning.

And I couldn't do it, couldn't go to school. I called in

sick. "Hello, I'm calling to say Taco Keller has fallen ill and he can't get up."

"Isn't this Taco?" the secretary asked.

"I'm my own guardian, and in my capacity as guardian, I'm telling you Taco Keller has fallen ill," I explained.

"Feel better," she said.

I slept until 2:00 p.m. without waking once. It felt like five minutes. At that point I got up and called Nussbaum to tell him I was super ill because my head ached and my body hurt.

He said, "You looked like shit on a cracker yesterday. We'd better talk about your future before you run yourself dead, amigo."

Then I slept again. The phone bleated like five times while I was in bed, but I couldn't get up to answer it. I was too far gone.

At 9:30 p.m., after I'd spent the better part of thirteen hours asleep, I stumbled into the kitchen, hoping to find something to eat. There was a dry hot dog bun in a cupboard but no hot dogs.

I cried a little bit and then walked down to the EZ shop in subzero temperatures. I spent $3.99 on two turbo dogs and a fountain Pepsi. They made me feel as sick as sick as could be, but at least I got some calories in me because I wouldn't get another paycheck for several days. I gave a fistful of that money to Maggie, and I had to pay for electricity and heat, which didn't leave me enough to live on.

Only when I got home did I realize there were all these messages on the answering machine, and these messages made me forget my selfish hunger and illness.

"Where are you?" Maggie cried in her first message. "Jared Chandler just called me 'whale mother.' I'm hiding in the costume loft. I need you here."

Twenty minutes later she'd called again. "Taco! Come to school!"

An hour later she'd said, "Why are people being so mean to me about being pregnant? Why don't they respect *life*, man?"

Like ten minutes later, she'd said, "Coach Millen just snagged me in the hall. She said we have to talk after school. I don't want to talk."

Coach Millen is the cheerleading coach. Didn't sound good.

And then finally, sometime later in the afternoon, she'd said, "I'm outside your house. Your door is locked. I rang the bell. I pounded, man. Where are you? Where are you? Don't abandon me!"

I slammed down the phone and ran to the front door, flinging the thing open and looking out into the snow, but of course, Maggie wasn't there. (Thank God because she would've been frozen to death on the lawn.) I must've been asleep so hard, dingus. I didn't hear the bell ringing or pounding or anything.

I called Maggie's cell, but it went straight to voice mail. "I'm here! I just got really sick and fell asleep for thirteen hours. Call me!"

Then I got on the computer and emailed Maggie.

Call me! Call me! Call me!

I waited by the phone for several hours, but there were no calls. There were no new emails either, except from Brad Schwartz, who wrote simply,

Uh-oh, dude. Pregnant???

I couldn't sleep—half because I'd slept all day, half because my body clock was all messed up from working nights, half because I was having surges of adrenaline, waiting for Maggie to contact me, and about a third because Ms. Carlson, the band director, had also left a message telling me I'd skipped a basketball game without excuse and they'd have to find another bass drummer if I couldn't be counted on, which made me want to puke.

Maggie finally emailed me at six o'clock the next

morning. I'd been hitting refresh for forty-five minutes when the message popped up. She wrote,

> It's way too late to get an abortion, Taco. I'm coming over there, and we're skipping school to talk because I need you to stand up and be a man and not think it's okay to sleep while I'm getting burnt at the stake like Hester Effing Prynne.

Burnt? Hester Prynne had to wear a big A. Nobody burned her! But that wasn't Maggie's point, was it?

I hurt in my forehead. I took a deep breath. I'd already skipped a day of school. Would another hurt? Did it even matter? Did anything matter if I was such a screwup?

Yes! My kid mattered. And wasn't I a dad, and didn't our (me and Maggie's) success as parents depend on me being available in times of need?

I wrote back,

> You got it, lady pal. I'll be here.

Maggie responded,

> Stop calling me that. Cut the bullshit, Taco.

Lady pal? Stop with lady pal? But that's what I called Maggie. How was that bullshit?

I went to the bathroom and stared in the mirror and promised myself I would cut the bullshit. Then I got in the shower and showered as hard as I could to try to wake myself up, but I was dizzy and very sad in my muscles, which is a really weird feeling. How can your muscles feel sad? They can. That's why I laid so still after Mom died. Because even though I couldn't cry, my muscles were so sad, they didn't want to move. Liquid sadness had pooled in them. I wanted to lie down in the shower too. So I sang *Wizard of Oz* songs to try to cheer up. But I was no longer the Mayor of Munchkinland, and my pregnant girlfriend felt like she was being burnt at the stake because I was a little bullshitty boy who couldn't even show up to school to protect her!

I toweled dry. Then I pulled my jams back on, slid on my bear-claw slippers, and sat down on the couch while I waited for Maggie to show up.

Maggie didn't show.

Then I waited another hour, pacing, staring out the window, opening the front door, and looking up and down the street.

Maggie didn't show.

By that time, both of us should've been in English.

Then I waited another hour, panicking until I thought I'd barf on the carpet like a drunken Darius.

But Maggie didn't show.

I began jogging from the kitchen to the living room and back again.

Right before calc was to start, Brad Schwartz called. "Where are you?" he asked. "What are you doing, man? Everybody says you quit school and ran away."

"I didn't run away!"

"Why are you out of breath?" he asked.

"I'm running in circles," I said.

"Run to school. Come to calc," Brad said.

"I can't. Maggie Corrigan is coming over, and we're going to be adults and talk about this baby like adults," I said.

"I just saw Maggie in the hall. She doesn't look like an adult. She looks like a kid who is pregnant with a kid."

"You saw her at school?"

"Yeah," Brad said. "What other hall would I be talking about?"

"Oh my God! I'll be right there!" I shouted.

Why did Maggie tell me to stay home and then go to school? I still don't know, dingus. But I'll tell you this: It caused me great consternation. Massive, crazy, energy-buzzing consternation, which, to be honest, wasn't smart

247

consternation. I slammed down the suite phone and took off for school as fast as I could. In fact, I bolted so fast, I was still wearing my PJ pants and my bear claw slippers. These furry slippers didn't keep me warm in the snow, not at all. Snow soaked my slippers. Snow froze my toes as I ran. My jams didn't keep me warm either. The wind blistered through the thin fabric and bit me on the butt. I ran down the hill and up to school.

Wearing this bedroom getup, I showed up shivering and red-faced and watery-eyed about ten minutes late for calc. I burst in the door. "Hi," I said too loud to Brad Schwartz and the rest of the class.

Mr. Edwards took one look at me, pointed at the door, and said, "No, Taco. No way. You go straight to the office."

Brad Schwartz looked scared.

"Okay, thanks," I said because I didn't really want to sit in calc anyway. In fact, I'm not even sure why I headed there in the first place. I guess because Brad called, right? Really, I wanted to know what the crap was going on with Maggie. That's why I'd run to school in my damn PJs.

I was on my way to Maggie's current events class when Dr. Evans, our principal, spotted me. "Stop, Taco. You come here right now."

But I didn't. I cut left and flew down a perpendicular

hall, slipping with every step in my wet bear slippers. (I fell once and whacked my knee, but I popped back up.) Dr. Evans must've taken off running too, but not after me. Ten seconds later just as I got to Mrs. Schoebel's room, an announcement boomed over the school intercom. It said, "Taco Keller, report to the office immediately. If any faculty or staff sees Taco Keller, please escort him to the office."

I didn't have a lot of time. I pounded on Schoebel's door like a mountain gorilla. Maggie looked up from her desk and sort of screamed, "Oh shit." Schoebel whipped open the door and grabbed the back of my neck in this Vulcan death grip. I tried to shake loose, but Schoebel is the volleyball coach, and the lady has some mad strength.

"Maggie!" I cried.

"I'm sorry! I'm sorry!" Maggie wailed, but she didn't get up out of her chair to help me.

Mrs. Schoebel dragged me down the hall. I couldn't stop her because my bear slippers have no traction (especially when they're soaked). I kept twisting around to see if Maggie would follow us, but she didn't. Coach Johnson ran up out of no place and grabbed my arm, and he kept me from twisting around.

These two big athletic teachers hurt my spirit, dingus. As they pulled, I said, "You can both let go, okay? I'm not fighting anymore. I'm going to the office." But neither of them let go, and neither of them said a word. Truth is, if they'd let go, I would totally have run back to Maggie.

Later, Nussbaum told me I could sue them for getting physical. But I liked Schoebel and Johnson a lot, and they were just doing their jobs, even if it hurt to get dragged by my neck and my arm at the same time.

They pulled me into the office, past the secretaries, who were all standing and flushed in their faces, and back to a little conference room. I backed into a corner, and they crowded in after me. Both Schoebel and Johnson were breathing really hard, and their faces were all sweaty. Mrs. Schoebel glared. Coach Johnson shook his head like he couldn't believe what he was seeing.

"What?" I couldn't take the pressure of all their eyeballs on me.

"What?" Coach Johnson spat. "What are you doing, Taco?" he shouted. "What in the hell are you thinking?"

"I don't know. I don't know!"

Mrs. Schoebel sighed. "I have to get back to my classroom."

"Tell Maggie I'm okay. Please!" I said.

"I'm not your messenger," Mrs. Schoebel spat. She glared again before she stepped out.

As she left, Dr. Evans came in. Dr. Evans and Coach

Johnson looked at each other for a moment. Then Dr. Evans turned to me. "So what is this?"

"I don't know," I said.

"No?" she asked.

"No," I said.

"I don't even know who to call, Taco. Your dad? The mental ward? You're wearing bear slippers and pajamas. You're breaking into classrooms? What are we supposed to do with you?"

"Why do you guys keep asking me questions? Why would you think I know what you're supposed to do? Clearly I don't know anything!"

"Calm down, Taco," Coach Johnson said. "Right now, kid, or else."

"Oh yeah? There we go again with the 'or else,'" I said. "Everybody says, 'Or else.' Or else what? Or else you'll kick my ass?"

"No," Dr. Evans said.

"Yes!" I shouted. "Dad says everybody wants to kick my ass and that you're just looking for an excuse! Well, here it is! Go ahead! Or else I'll keep taking care of my baby!"

Dr. Evans blinked a couple times. Then she said, "Taco, I don't want to hurt you. Nobody here does."

"Or else!" I cried. "Or else!"

Dr. Evans said quietly, "No, we won't hurt you, Taco. You have to calm down or else we can't protect you. Do you understand?"

"Protect me from what?"

"Yourself, Taco, because your behavior warrants more serious intervention—police intervention—that could really mess up your life."

The police? No, dingus. No. "Cops," I said. I took some deep breaths. I nodded. I tried to blow out all the pain in my chest. I sucked in air and tried to talk calmly. "Calm down or else I'm a criminal. Is that it?"

Dr. Evans nodded. "That's what we mean."

I nodded again. I breathed more. "A real top-grade delinquent? Like a public enemy?" My voice cracked.

Dr. Evans nodded again.

I exhaled long and slow. "No," I said. "I'm just me. Seriously."

Dr. Evans nodded. She reached out and put her hand on my arm. "Now who do I call?"

"Um," I said. "I can't say. I don't know. Could I have a minute to compose myself? I don't really know how to answer your question, but I don't want you to call the police or the mental ward."

"Okay," Dr. Evans said really quietly.

"You want me to go too?" Coach Johnson asked.

"Yes, sir. I'm sorry," I said.

"You won't do anything stupid if you're alone, will you?" Coach Johnson asked.

"No, I'll just sit here for a few minutes. I swear. I'm just me."

"I'll be right outside this door," Dr. Evans said to Coach.

"Well, okay," he said and left. Dr. Evans left too, and it was me in my Taco cage, dingus.

Whoa. Who is the *real* dingus? Just call me Mr. Dingles.

After maybe twenty minutes of sitting and taking deep breaths, during which I couldn't conjure up the voice of my mom or the image of the Tibet baby for guidance, I couldn't really think of any adult who'd care enough to deal with me. (I couldn't have them call my dad because I hated his guts for what he was doing to me and Darius.) I decided I had two choices. One, I could ask to be released on my own reconnaissance, which seemed like a long shot. Two, I could ask them to call Mr. Nussbaum, even though he was just my boss at my job that didn't pay money. At least he seemed official since he's a lawyer.

I also thought about climbing into a heating vent to escape. Except I wouldn't ever be able to come back to school, and I wanted to learn, not become a criminal.

I stood and tried to leave to find Dr. Evans, but I'd been locked in the room, which seemed reasonable. So I knocked quietly but loud enough to be heard by somebody in the office. A second later, Dr. Evans opened the door and sat down at the table across from me.

"Are you composed?" she asked.

"I am. I'm not going to try to break out like Jason Bourne," I said.

"That's a relief. Is there someone I should call now?"

"Well, it's complicated, Dr. Evans. I'm pretty much alone in the world, and maybe that's part of my problem. If Mom were around, I know this wouldn't be happening. But she's not around, and it is happening."

Dr. Evans nodded solemnly. "I liked your mom."

"Yeah. Uh-huh," I said. "Given that I'm alone in the world, my preference would be for you to not call anybody. If things were different, I might have asked you to call Darius, but my brother is already beyond the 'or else' stage. I don't want to go there."

Dr. Evans nodded. "You *are* already in trouble though, correct? I understand you're the father of Maggie Corrigan's baby. Is that true?"

"Yeah, we didn't mean to make a baby. But we did it. You know…*it*. A lot," I said.

"Okay," Dr. Evans said. "You're not in jail, but

254

doesn't that baby make you beyond the 'or else' stage in a different way, Taco? Aren't you in over your head?"

"Oh," I said. "Huh." I thought for a moment and tried to answer that question as honestly as I could, and it seemed to me that I answered truthfully. "I don't think so. I have a job, so I make some money. And I have a nice bedroom, so the baby could live with me, and I could definitely be its best pal. We could go to the swimming pool, and we could go running in the park—you know, do some swinging and have goofy little kid dance parties. I'd be the best dad."

Dr. Evans was very calm and quiet when she replied. "You just described being a great big brother, not a dad, Taco. You'd be a perfect big brother to any kid. I know it."

"No, dads do that stuff. And feed the kid too."

"How would you instruct your…let's say your son… if his girlfriend couldn't see him anymore? Would you suggest he go over to her house to climb it? Would you tell him to secretly meet her to have sex in private parts of the school?"

"Me and Maggie never had sex in the school," I said. "Never!"

"Did you take off your clothes?"

"Well…how do you know about that?"

"Don Jackson swears he saw you two naked when he

255

was mopping the stage, but when I got to the costume loft to investigate, it was locked. Did you take off your clothes in the costume loft, Taco? Be honest."

"Yeah, a few times. But I'd never tell my kid to do that, okay? And I wouldn't tell him to climb a house. I'm not dumb."

"You're not dumb, Taco. You're so bright in many ways. But you aren't always smart in other ways."

"Yeah." I nodded. "Okay, that's true." Really, I knew that, dingus. There was plenty of evidence.

"Not that it's terminal. It won't be like that forever. You're just not acting smart now because you have a kid's brain tucked in an adult's body. Some things that seem like good ideas—and maybe are good ideas for a kid— are terrible ideas for an adult."

"Really?" I said.

"Really," Dr. Evans said. "Do you want your child to be affected by your appropriately immature decision making?"

"Oh, crap, no. Of course not," I said.

"I'm sorry," she said.

I put my hand on my forehead because it felt hot. "I don't like this," I said.

Dr. Evans smiled. Then she said, "You know, your brother, Darius, is in the same boat, Taco. He looks like an adult, but he's not ready to be an adult. Maybe there's been a little too much pressure on the both of you since your mother died. Have you ever considered that?"

"No," I said. "But yeah, that could be true."

"Okay," Dr. Evans said. "Here's what I'm going to do, and I need you to go along with it...or else. Got it?"

"Yeah," I said. "Or else. I get it. Thank you."

"I'm going to send you home today. I want you to stay there and be quiet. Call your dad if you want. Call Sergeant Frederick if you need to. I saw him at the grocery store over the weekend, and he wanted to know how you were doing, so he'd be a good person to call if you're comfortable talking to him."

I offered, "I could talk to Mr. Nussbaum. He's nice to me."

Dr. Evans paused over that. "The lawyer?"

I nodded.

Then she said, "Or Coach Johnson maybe? You can call me too, if I seem like the right person to talk to. But, Taco, you spend the rest of the day thinking about what's happened and what comes next for you. Sort things out. I want you back here tomorrow and Friday to serve an in-school suspension. I'll make sure you have the assignments you need from your classes so you'll be up to date. If it goes well, I'll let you attend classes regularly on Monday."

I leaned forward and asked the only question that was dangling out there in front of me. "What do you want me to sort out exactly?"

"This situation with you wanting to be a father. Ask yourself a lot of questions. Do some hard thinking, Taco. What do you really want? You're not going to be a playmate or a brother. You're going to be a father. Make sure you understand what that really means—the consequences for both you and a baby. I'm concerned that you're not seeing things exactly as they are. This isn't a mental health diagnosis, okay? It's developmentally appropriate. Do you understand?"

"No?" I said.

"Okay, Taco. Listen. You're a bit delusional, which is charming when the stakes are low but potentially disastrous when they're not."

I sat back and thought for a moment. And then it hit me. "Oh, I totally get it. Just like Mr. Corrigan said. This is really real."

"Yes," Dr. Evans said. "It really is."

CHAPTER 28

That whole afternoon, Maggie Corrigan called and called the suite. She left like a hundred and twenty messages in three hours, but I didn't pick up. I guess she got kicked out of cheerleading because one of the rules in the athletic contract includes, "Don't get knocked up." I felt bad because she was really upset and she wanted to talk. She said she was worried about me, which maybe she was. But I didn't answer, and I didn't call her back. Instead I locked the door so I could think without my pregnant girlfriend barging in to stop me from sorting out my business.

I pulled out all the things I'd made or written out about the baby, all the drawings, the notes on calendars, the calculations, etc. I studied them.

Made me sad. Seemed reasonable that this stuff would make me sad.

I stared out the window for a long time. I really thought.

Around four, instead of walking over to Nussbaum's office, I called him. I didn't call to tell him I wasn't coming in. I called to thank him for being nice when my own dad had apparently abandoned me and my brother.

He paused for a few seconds after that and then asked, "Where are you, amigo?"

"At home."

"You don't want to come to the office to talk?" he asked.

"There was a little trouble at school, and Dr. Evans said I need to stay here and think."

"How's that working for you?" he asked.

"Pretty good," I said. "I'm calm anyway." It was pretty weird because Mom used to say exactly that when she was checking in on me. *How's that working for you?*

"Did this school trouble have anything to do with Maggie Corrigan?" he asked.

"Yeah. Something. Everything," I said. I sat down at the dining room table and picked up the picture of the wise lion I'd made for Maggie in the fall, the one I thought I'd paint on the suite wall. I shook my head. *So stupid.*

"You go ahead and think. How about I take you out for a doughnut before school tomorrow morning?"

"Yeah, Mr. Nussbaum. Sounds good."

And it did sound good. I really like Mr. Nussbaum, even if Emily Cook's dad says he's a scoundrel and the mention of his name caused Dr. Evans to lose her train of thought.

I felt pretty good hanging up the phone. There was something to look forward to. Doughnut with old Nussbaum. But the feeling of stability didn't last because right then somebody tried to come in the house. I could hear the creak as the screen door swung open. I dropped to the floor and crawled into the hall, heart pounding. Someone twisted and jiggled the doorknob. *Oh crap*, I thought. I was certain it was Maggie Corrigan, and I couldn't talk to her because I knew that she made me delusional. Seriously! My love for her made me crazy, right? I want to drink her. I want to swim like a dolphin with her. I had to be alone. I had to follow Dr. Evans's advice. The screen door crashed shut and then reopened.

I stayed in the hall, where there are no windows she might see me through. I waited, barely able to catch my breath. The person rattled the doorknob again and pounded. I slid down flat on the floor and rolled up into a little Taco ball.

Then I heard, "Aw shit, please!" from the doorstep.

I couldn't believe it. It was Darius.

I ran to open the door. He stood on the step in dark blue sweats and his coat.

"Oh Christ, Darius. You didn't escape from prison, did you?"

Darius shook his head as he pushed past me into the house. "No, I guess they let people out pretty quick for good behavior. They only have like ten beds up there, so there isn't enough room to keep dumb drunks for their whole sentences."

"You've only been gone ten days," I said. "I…I don't know. Is that enough time?"

He pulled off his coat and dropped it on the floor. "Yeah."

"Good," I said, although I really wasn't sure. "So I guess you behaved well?"

"I didn't fight with anybody. I watched TV, and I didn't talk, so I behaved well."

"That's great!"

Darius glared at me. "Cut the shit, man. Cut the shit right now."

"Okay. I'm sorry. I'm just glad you're out."

"I bet. Now I can make money to keep you warm and fed, right?"

"No," I said. "I'm glad you're free." Then I hugged him, and he went limp like a dead fish.

"I gotta go to bed now," he said. "Let go of me."

Darius went downstairs and passed out, and I relocked the front door.

The rest of the afternoon there were three phone calls

and three knocks at the door, but I didn't answer. I just hunkered down in the hall where no one could see me. I meditated on my situation. At five thirty, when it was dark, I decided I could leave the house. I decided I had to.

I exited, carrying a pillow and my blanket.

No, dingus, I wasn't heading over to Maggie Corrigan's for a sleepover. Even though it was a Wednesday and not my shift, I headed to the hospital. How about this? I'd signed up Maggie and me for the birth class, and the first session was that night.

And no, dingus, I wasn't going because of my capacity for delusion. I was going because—I'd come up with this while hanging in the hall—what better place to figure out what it means to be a dad than a birth class?

The instructions in the class brochure said that each couple had to bring a pillow and blanket. That's why I carried that through the polar bear night.

Mrs. Poller, my boss, sat at a little decorated card table next to the hospital reception desk. When I entered, carrying that pillow and blanket, she looked pretty confused.

"Hi, there," I said. "Here for my class."

"I saw that you were on the list. William Keller and partner? That's Maggie Corrigan, I'm going to assume? I believe she's pregnant, isn't she?" Ms. Poller sounded all weird and skeptical.

"Uh, yeah. I don't think she'll be joining me though," I said.

"Oh," Ms. Poller said.

I checked out the decorations festooning the table. There were little baby booties and some tiny diapers and a little baby beanie that some grandma must've knitted, and there were a bunch of baby pictures on a poster board. (*Alumni*, said the caption.) And there was a little plastic first-aid kit filled with baby shampoo bottles and some Q-tips and a little thing of rubbing alcohol and some kind of ointment in a squeeze tube.

"What's the muck in the squeeze tube for?" I asked.

"Diaper rash," Ms. Poller said.

"Ouch," I said. "Poor kids get their butts burned by poop, huh?"

"Yes." Ms. Poller nodded. Then she said in a whisper, "This class really is for couples, Taco."

"Do you mind if I just attend as an observer then? Dr. Evans up at school would like me to sort things out, so I'm trying."

Ms. Poller smiled and swallowed hard. "Taco," she said, "you just break my heart."

"I'm sorry." I didn't know what else to say.

"You'll be meeting in the common room. Several couples are in there already. Go ahead," Ms. Poller said.

Usually there are institutional lunch tables in the common room, but they were all folded up and pushed to the side. At the front of the room, there was a screen with a projector showing a baby inside a belly. For whatever reason, the kid looked like Darius, which was weird. Same facial expression.

The other couples were sitting on the floor on their blankets, and there was an iPod plugged into the projector speakers playing some yoga music, the kind Mom listened to when Dad would get pissed and head out to Toby's Tap for beers. Two of the couples looked relaxed, but one of the guys in another couple was all jumpy, making stupid jokes. I'd actually seen this guy at the roller skating rink when I was a kid. He was an employee, the "skate cop" back then. He'd roll around acting cool, and he'd make lots of dumb jokes and stop teens from making out too hard by the snack stand. Didn't seem like he'd changed much. His wife or girlfriend or whatever kept whispering to him in a voice you could totally hear. "Just stop, Craig. Calm down."

Two more couples came in after me and put their stuff on the floor, so I put my blanket on the floor too, and yes, dingus, the couples all stared at me. One woman asked, "Are you here for school or something?"

"Yeah," I said. "Trying to figure this whole deal out." It seemed like I was telling the truth, even if my original plan was to be on a baby team with Maggie. A minute later, a woman with long hair, yoga pants, and clogs came into the room. ("Hippie," that dude Craig whispered.) She said, "Welcome, welcome!" Ms. Poller came in too and handed everybody questionnaires to fill out, which included a section about what health insurance we'd be using to cover the class and delivery.

"I don't know anything about insurance," I whispered to her.

"Don't worry about it," Ms. Poller said. "You're just observing."

Then the yoga pants lady said, "I'm Jo, the nurse practitioner who will be leading you through the next month. I'm so happy you've decided to take this class. Giving birth can be stressful, right?"

"Right," a few women agreed.

"The idea is that we'll get ready for any possibility. We'll control what we can control. We'll get to know the things we can't. We'll give those things up to whatever our higher power is, and we'll keep the stress low. Daddies, that's your main job, okay? Lower the stress."

Craig raised his hand.

"Yes?" Jo asked.

"So after the baby comes, how much time do we have to wait before we can get it on again?"

"You mean resume a normal sex life?" Jo asked.

"He's worried his junk will turn blue and fall off," his partner said.

"Oh, honey," Jo said with fake sadness. "You're going to be fine."

"I don't know. Ha-ha," said Craig.

Some of the other moms-to-be and dads shook their heads at him.

Introductions followed. Everybody seemed a little nervous. I said I was observing for school. Craig made some more lame jokes about forgetting his condoms or whatever. Then the conversation swirled into basics: vaginal tearing during birth (got me dizzy) and some kind of surgical cutting called an episiotomy (made my mouth water like I might puke) and then into this, like, oil massaging that the ladies (or their partners) could do on some lady part called the perineum that might help that part be more supple and rubbery or whatever, which would keep it in shape and make it less likely to tear and make it more likely that the lady will be ready for more sex on the early end of things. Just in case the dad's junk is turning blue and is in danger of falling off. And right then and there I barfed on the floor.

"Oh, honey!" Jo exclaimed.

"Oh, gross!" the woman next to me bellowed.

"Wait till he sees the birth videos!" Craig cried.

"Oh God. Oh man. I'm so sorry. It's not about the women parts, okay?"

"I don't think you're ready for this, honey," Jo said, standing up. "Katie! Katie!"

Then I started crying, which you know I don't really do, dingus.

Another of the men leaned toward me and said, "I'm not interested in sex right now, kid. I just want my daughter to be healthy. That's why I'm here. We're not all like that guy."

"Okay." I hiccupped. "Okay." That was good. I needed to hear that.

Then the night janitor came flying in with a mop and bucket, followed by Ms. Poller, who helped me clean myself up out in the hall. I'd barfed mostly on my blanket, and she said she'd put it in the hospital laundry for me to pick up the next day at my shift. After that she said, "I don't want you to go back in there, Taco."

"I won't barf again. Promise. That Craig guy just made me really sad, but the other guy is nice. I'll be fine."

"No, they're going to watch videos of difficult births."

"I can handle it. I've seen all kinds of blood since I've worked here."

"That Craig fellow is going to make more bad jokes.

I know his type. You'll get to know his type too. But I can't have you freaking out in the class, Taco. These new parents really need calm."

"Why would he make jokes?"

"Because that's how some people respond to difficult situations. By making dumb jokes. It's a defense mechanism."

I exhaled and put my head in my hands. "I think I kind of do that sometimes."

"You're going to be okay."

I looked up at her. "I'm not ready for this, Ms. Poller."

"For what?"

"Just everything, you know? I have the maturity level of Craig, except it doesn't make him barf to be that way."

"It probably should," Ms. Poller said.

"Yeah, well, it doesn't, and what does that mean?"

"Adults can be awful," Ms. Poller said.

"This is real," I said. I shook my head. "I need some water."

CHAPTER 29

I was only gone from the suite for a couple hours, but that was enough time for Darius to turn into a destroyer. As I walked up the block to the house, I sensed something was wrong. The front inside door was wide open. *Has Darius gone stupid? He knows how much that heat is going to cost!* I thought.

I burst in through the screen door all ready to lose my mind at Darius for leaving the interior door ajar, but what I found was that Darius had already lost his. He sat in the middle of the floor in the living room. Behind him, Dad's old recliner had been turned over. In front of him was a giant pile of ripped up paper and photos. He had a bottle of Jack Daniel's to his left that was two-thirds empty. He must've been chugging. He also had scissors and a steak knife lying on the carpet on his right. He held up an old photo album, and he was tearing out the pages.

"Shit, man!" I shouted. "What are you doing?"

"Getting rid of this crap," Darius said. "Bullshit is holding us back. I really do got bad blood in my veins, dude. Comes from these bad people." He pointed at a picture of our young Mom and Dad.

I rushed across the room and grabbed the album out of his hand.

"No! Stop that!"

The album was an old one from Mom's parents. I stared at its wreckage for a second. Then I threw it like a Frisbee across the room to get it away from him. I fell down onto my knees and swept up a pile of trashed pictures from in front of him. "Crap. Shit," I said, looking at the ripped-off heads of my relatives and my parents. "Why?"

"Why, pie, sky, fry," Darius said, smiling. "You ass face."

He'd already ruined Mom and Dad's wedding album—the one that had all the dead people I loved pretty much like I remembered them, the one I looked at when I felt sad or sometimes when I felt happy because it made me feel warm and full of love to see my parents and Grandpa and Grandma and Dad's dead brother so happy and dancing and eating cake while dressed up like it was a royal occasion. "Oh shit. You idiot!" I cried. I showed him a ripped picture of our grandma. "You assassin!"

Darius paused and blinked at me. "Aw, come on, Taco," he said. "I'm doing this for you too! Got to take care of our little boy!"

Clearly jail hadn't done Darius any good. It made him worse. Not just a drunk. A psycho.

He reached for the album that I'd tossed away from him. Adrenaline exploded in me. I jumped into the air and landed on him, catching his arm at an awkward angle on the couch. There was a crazy popping noise, and Darius started screaming.

"Oh shit." I pushed off him so I wouldn't kill him more, but my shove just made him screech louder.

"Stop! Don't hurt me! Ahhh!"

I rolled onto my knees and hovered over him. "Darius, I think you broke your arm or shoulder or something. We have to take you to the hospital."

"Don't be nice to me. You weren't even in Taco Bell, but I wanted you dead! I was so mad," Darius cried. "I'm sorry!"

"What?" I couldn't believe it. Did Darius really just say that? Did he mean it?

"It's not you. It's them!" He pointed at the pile of photo albums. "They gave me my bad blood. You didn't. I'm sorry. I'm sorry. I'm sorry." Darius sobbed and rolled up into a ball.

"I'm going to call the ambulance."

"Don't!" he bellowed. "I can't be drunk! They'll call jail! I'll go back!"

"Oh Jesus," I said. "You need help, Darius."

"Don't call Dad!" he cried.

I took a deep breath. *Hold on*, I thought. *Hold on. Hold on.* "Okay. I won't call Dad. But we need a real adult." I got up as calmly as I could and called Nussbaum's cell from the suite's landline.

By the time Nussbaum got to our place, it was getting close to midnight. He said he had to take care of a couple things before he came over. He was slurring when he said it, and I figured from the background noise that he was playing cards at the VFW when I called. He still smelled a little like cigars when he arrived, but he didn't slur. He held a cup of QuikTrip coffee in his hand. I almost hugged him.

Darius lay on the couch, passed out cold. In between my call and Nussbaum's arrival, I held a trash can to catch Darius's barf and tried to tell him stories from books I'd read for English. I almost called the ambulance twice because of all the barfing. But he begged me not to. "Don't make me go back there," he cried. I was so relieved when he went to sleep, but I slapped him every five minutes to make sure he wasn't unconscious. He'd had so much of that stupid whiskey.

"Well, well, amigo," Mr. Nussbaum said when he arrived. "I wasn't expecting to see you until our doughnut breakfast. Looks like things took a turn for the worse?"

"No joke," I said.

"Huh. The county's putting petty criminals and drunks back on the street as fast as they can. Looks like Darius could've used a bit more lockup time to consider his options," Nussbaum said.

"Can jail really fix a guy like that?"

Nussbaum stared at my broken brother. "No, my friend. Darius needs something different than jail."

"Like serious prison maybe?" I started to lose it because Nussbaum being there meant I could. "Maybe he should just be locked away forever. He's a lost cause. I think he was trying to kill me when he ran into the Taco Bell," I said.

Nussbaum said really quietly, "Can't let that happen, amigo. No murders. Well, what's next?"

Nussbaum stepped over to Darius and slapped him a couple times on the face—sort of like I had before, not hard.

Darius said groggily, "Stop doing that, man. Okay?" Then he lolled back asleep.

Nussbaum turned to me. "Doesn't seem to be in danger of dying from booze at the moment, although his time's coming if he doesn't get straightened out." Nussbaum stared at the ceiling for a moment and then continued. "He's had repeated alcohol-related trouble, growing in severity. Not good. I've seen this before, you know? Joys of being a lawyer. The kid needs some chemical treatment, some real rehab, and mental health counseling."

"Yeah," I said. "He has adult problems but a kid's brain. He's not prepared for any of this shit, Nussbaum."

Mr. Nussbaum nodded. "Sound familiar by any chance?"

I nodded.

"You get some sleep, amigo. I'll take first shift, making sure your doofus brother doesn't choke on his own puke. We'll take him to the hospital when he's sober so he doesn't get slammed for breaking the conditions of his early release. Sound like a plan?"

"Uh-huh. Okay. Great," I said. I almost told Mr. Nussbaum that I loved him, which would've been super weird. Instead I went back to the master suite and passed out cold because I was destroyed.

Mr. Nussbaum's "first shift" lasted the whole night.

I slept hard. And I think I had a dream with a Tibet baby or maybe about my mom tucking me into bed, but it was all hazy when I woke up, so I can't really tell for sure.

275

CHAPTER 30

A weird smell woke me. The morning light slid in through the window as I pried open my sleepy eyes. Light? In January in the state of Wisconsin, that meant it was already past seven in the morning. *What about my shift to watch Darius? Was Nussbaum asleep? Had Darius choked on his own poison?*

I rolled out of bed fast, heart accelerating, and ran out into the living room. Nussbaum sat there in Dad's recliner, smoking one of his stinky cigars. His shoes and socks were off and so was his tie. Darius slept on the couch.

"Oh, you're making that stink," I said.

He ignored me. "Taco, goddamn it, there's not a stitch of food in this whole house. How in the hell are you staying alive, kid?"

"I really don't know," I said.

Nussbaum nodded at me. "Sit down for a few minutes, would you?"

I sat down on the love seat. It's my favorite chair. Love seat means a two-butt couch, and my mom bought it right before she was diagnosed with ovarian cancer, so I think of it as Mom's love in a seat. "What's up?" I asked.

"Your brother was awake for a while. We had a nice chat," Nussbaum said. "He really was thinking about you when he hit the Taco Bell. How about that?"

"Why didn't he just hit me?" I asked. "Would've cost less."

"Because he doesn't actually want to hurt you, so he got loaded and then took out his anger on the Taco Bell." He paused. "I don't think Darius can do outpatient treatment. I'm familiar with different levels of alcohol use."

"Right. Because you're an expert about... Because you're a lawyer," I said.

"Well, I'll be honest with you, son, I've got a bit of a reputation as a drinker myself. I enjoy my cards, and my wife's been dead for twenty years."

"You're too young to have a dead wife for that long," I said.

"She was far too young when she died, Taco." Nussbaum took a deep breath. "Anyway, I drink a little. What else am I going to do?"

"Take a walk in the woods? Go to a movie? Take a trip to Tibet?" I suggested.

"Yeah, sure. Alone? My only family's at the VFW.

That's where I go. And the people who count know I enjoy myself, but I'm safe and smart. I don't drive unless I'm sober, and when I work, I work like a dog."

"Hound dog," I said.

"Right you are," Nussbaum replied. "But this kid?" He pointed with his thumb at snoring Darius. "This kid doesn't want to exist right now. He's not safe. He said the only thing he could think of while he was in jail was drinking himself unconscious. He needs help, but he won't make it through outpatient treatment. He'll leave a meeting and go right to a liquor store. I guarantee it. Getting treatment and getting healthy is a hard business, and this kid's as soft as dough."

"Okay?" I said.

"Not okay," Nussbaum said. "I don't know what kind of insurance your waste of a father carries, but I'm guessing it's no good. Inpatient treatment could run you fifty grand or more, if we're talking three months of it, which is what I expect Darius needs."

"Oh Jesus! Where am I going to get that kind of money?" I asked. "Darius already owes a boatload in fines and crap for trying to kill Taco Bell! And I make three hundred dollars every two weeks at the hospital!"

Nussbaum swallowed hard. "Three hundred dollars? Is that right?"

"Yeah. It's a lot, but it doesn't add up unless I can get more shifts. Maybe I can get some more shifts?"

Nussbaum sighed. He shook his head. "Taco?"

"Yeah?"

"I hope you know I have your best interest at heart, but I'm going to say something you might not want to hear, all right?"

"I don't need any more bad news, okay?"

"You have to hear this right now," Nussbaum said.

I sighed. "Fine. Go for it."

"You are not in any way ready to be a daddy."

I looked down at the floor. "I know that," I said. "But is anybody ready? Craig at my birth class just wants to have sex all the time, not be a dad."

"Who the hell's Craig?"

"You know that roller-skating guy? Kind of old?"

"You mean Craig Colstad? Owns Roller World?"

"He owns it? He's a dipshit. He's definitely not ready for a baby."

"Probably true. But he has money. He also has an adult wife," Nussbaum said.

"That was his wife?"

"That's right, amigo. And Connie Colstad has inner resources. Craig Colstad has money. You don't have either. Taco, three hundred dollars isn't anything. Three hundred dollars won't even keep *you* in food. What about the baby's food and diapers and heat and electricity and rent? And there's medical and dental and toys and clothes… You can't believe how fast those little buggers grow out of their clothes! Sometimes in a week. Boy, I'll tell you—"

"Wait! Do you have kids, Mr. Nussbaum?"

"Well, yeah. A daughter."

"Where is she?" I couldn't believe it. Why didn't she talk to him? Did he do something terrible to her? Was this why some people think Nussbaum's a bad person? "You never mentioned her."

Mr. Nussbaum sighed. He seemed to get two sizes smaller, dingus. He swallowed hard. "She died in the same wreck that took my wife. Back in 1995. It was snowing. Truck slid through an intersection on 151. Took them both in a blink. That's why I won't drive until the roads are plowed. Makes me sick even now."

I could barely talk, I felt so bad. "I didn't know that. I'm so sorry, Nussbaum. I didn't know any—"

"That's not what we're talking about, amigo," Nussbaum said. "We're talking about you and your life and how you're going to get enough money to send this brother of yours to treatment."

"Okay," I whispered.

"First, Taco, you need to think like a real father. Protect that kid the best way you can. You need to sign that paper, sign away your parental rights. Your baby should grow up with capable parents who have resources. Do you understand?"

Even though I did, it hurt to say it. It felt like getting stabbed in my heart. "I do," I whispered. "I agree."

"Good," Nussbaum said. "Secondly, we need to deal with your brother. You don't have enough money to take care of him."

"No," I said.

"Now listen to me, amigo. You're going to sign that paper because you love your baby, right?"

"Right."

"The Corrigans will pay a lot of money for you to sign that paper. You can use that money to save your brother."

"But…I can't sell my baby."

"You aren't selling your baby. You are saving two *babies*." Nussbaum nodded at Darius. "This brother of yours needs you."

I looked at Darius. He was one beat-up baby. My mom's baby.

"Darius was your keeper after your mom died, correct, amigo?"

I nodded.

"Now it's your turn to take care of him."

I squinted. I thought. Nussbaum had piled the albums Darius hadn't destroyed in the corner. Those albums were all filled with people I loved—true. Those albums were filled with people who were gone. Darius snored on the couch. He was here. He had tried so hard for me. "I'm the keeper now," I said. "We need money for my brother."

"Okay," Nussbaum said. "You're in, Taco? You want me to get that money?"

"Yes, please."

"Good. Good thinking, kid. Now get your ass to school. You have a deal to fulfill with that principal of yours, correct?"

"Uh-huh," I said.

"I'll work the Corrigans through their lawyer. Don't say a word about this to Maggie. Don't say a word to her about anything. You understand?"

"Okay," I whispered.

Darius shifted on the couch, groaned. "I have to go to a doctor," he mumbled. "My arm, man."

"I'll take care of him too," Nussbaum said.

It was only eight in the morning, but it didn't feel like my best day. I would really rather dance on a stage or go running through the park or go to the pool for a good swim because that stuff doesn't hurt. But I wanted to make sure my baby and my mom's baby, Darius, would have good days, great days.

In the end, maybe that is what a best day looks like? Making hard decisions so that the people you love are okay?

CHAPTER 31

I walked into school as fast as I could. I heard Brad call for me, and probably Sharma too, but I just gave the thumbs-up and charged toward the office. I wasn't sure that Dr. Evans wanted me talking to anyone while I was serving in-school suspension. And I sincerely didn't want to talk to anyone either. I wasn't ready.

Dr. Evans was waiting for me in the office. "Did you reflect and sort things out, Taco?" Dr. Evans asked as she led me into the jail/suspension room.

"You don't even know how much."

"That's good," she said.

She told me I was welcome to use the computer for schoolwork, that she'd bring in lunch at 12:10, and that I should talk to a secretary if I needed to use the bathroom. Then she left me by myself with my assignments.

I started with calc, but it didn't make any sense. I looked at English. It was a study guide for the semester final, which was scheduled for the following week. The first question was about *Lord of the Flies*.

1. Some commentators call *Lord of the Flies* an allegory. If that is true, what message does Golding convey to his readers? What allegorical roles are the characters playing?

I got on the computer and looked up *allegory*. That helped me remember the term from class. An allegory is a story where the characters and events are symbols that stand for ideas about life. I thought, *Shit...*Lord of the Flies *is symbolic of my life.* And that's when it became totally clear, dingus. I had to write Maggie Corrigan to explain what was almost unexplainable—my newfound belief that we couldn't be together in this life because of our lack of inner resources and our childishness and our total *Lord of the Flies* bloodlust for touching each other.

Instead of doing the English study guide, I stayed on the computer, and I wrote:

January 13

Dear Maggie, who I will always love no matter what,

I'm stuck in a room here in school. Detention for trying to break into your classroom. You might think I'd be sad about detention, but I'm not because I needed a time-out. I need rules to stop me from harming myself and other people, including people I love (including you). What's weird about this is I don't mean harm. I only mean to be good and kind and to enjoy life. To me, enjoying life meant spending every minute I possibly could with you because you are definitely all the amazing things I've said you are during our relationship. You made me so happy, Maggie. Like, legitimately happy! So happy I want to drink you from a big cup!

Yeah, I have problems. Some of it comes from this: My mom died, and I didn't cry because I didn't think she wanted to see me cry. She loved how happy I was all the time. And really, I am a happy person, you know? She made me promise to say that every day was the best day I ever had, and I took that to mean I had to bullshit, to lie to myself and those around me to keep showing my happy face even when I wasn't happy. Best day ever!

My desire to actually be as happy as I
acted led me to get even more separated
from reality, I guess. It led me to think I
was capable of building a happy family
with you. You are a great dancer and a
great cheerleader! You make me laugh!
Why wouldn't you be the perfect wife
and mom?

Answer: Because, like me, you're kind of
a little kid, not a mom or a wife. You've
been angry in your life, and I think that's
why you agreed to try to be a family. (Like
maybe I could solve your anger.) It was a
bad idea, Maggie. You actually know this
better than me, I bet. You're very smart.

The great thing is our baby will make
another family really happy. Our baby is
going to be awesome. Can you imagine
a kid with your smarts and athletic ability
matched with my winning personality? Our
kid will make those adoptive parents, those
people with adult-sized inner resources,
the luckiest parents on the planet. I do
believe that.

In *Lord of the Flies*, lots of the kids thought

having no rules would be great fun. They ended up murdering one another. I want rules. I want someone to tell me what to do. I want to know where my next meal is coming from. But being around you makes me act like one of those crazy kids. You make me feel like a wild sexy monkey who wants to swing from the trees all day long. Clearly I'm not dad material at the moment. You're a mom biologically but not in your brain. Oh, Mags. I'm signing all the legal documents. I agree with your parents. I want their laws. We can't be parents, and we need to be apart. I will stay away. I do this because I love you and because I love me too.

Does all this make me sad? Yes. I already miss our perfect baby. I miss you so much, it hurts in my throat and my elbows and knees.

Does that mean this is a bad day? No. I only realized this very recently. My mom actually didn't say every day is your happiest day. She said every day is your best day. Sad days can be good days. Today I pledge to take care of you, me, and our baby. To do so, I must say good-bye. It's such a sad day, but it's still the best day ever because we're all alive and that means we can do good stuff and that's amazing—whether it's sad stuff or happy stuff. I think that's what my mom meant by best day ever. We can do good stuff every day we're alive no matter what.

I will love you forever, Maggie.

Sincerely,

William (Taco) Keller

It took me until lunch to type that on the computer because I'm a shit typer. And because I had to reread it a few times to make sure that my letter told Maggie what was in my heart. But I did it. Then I cut and pasted it into an email, and I sent it to her.

The rest of the afternoon, I pretended to study calc, but I just sort of cried. I thought about Maggie and my mom and Darius and my dad, and I hoped he and Miz had a good and adult relationship. And I wished everyone but Darius good-bye because I was letting them all go, except for Darius.

I am my brother's keeper.

That night, I called Emily Cook and asked her to take my hospital shift. She told me she would, and she told me she was sorry she'd been mean to me because clearly I was dealing with troubles I had no capacity to be dealing with, and it wasn't fair of her to pile on like that, even if I'd hurt her feelings by kissing Maggie Corrigan right in front of her.

I said, "You talk like a straight shooter, like my mom, which I appreciate."

She paused for a second or two, took a deep breath, and asked me to go to a movie in Dubuque sometime.

I told her I was a broken shell of a human, but I'd like that. As long as she didn't want to have sex.

She said, "You are weirder than anyone on earth." However, she did agree to my condition.

The next day Bluffton got hit by the snowstorm of the decade—twenty-two fat inches. That badass snow kept me shoveling for, like, fifteen hours. Darius couldn't help because his shoulder was beyond dislocated. It was broken. I sort of felt bad about it, but not really because it meant he had to sit still and reflect on all that had happened.

There was no school, and we had no food. Very late in the day after the roads were plowed the best they could be, Mr. Nussbaum braved the snow and brought us a pizza.

Darius had already agreed to check into Tellurian up in Madison. It didn't take much talking. Nussbaum said, "You need to be in treatment."

Darius said, "You know it, dude."

"Madison is the place."

"Anywhere," Darius said. "Please."

The next day Mr. Nussbaum got the money for Darius, and I signed the documents releasing my parental rights to the baby, even though it made me barf into the garbage pail next to Nussbaum's desk. I wasn't as sad about the baby itself. I really did believe it would have better parents than me. I was sick because Maggie couldn't just sign a paper and be done. She would carry it with her and get bigger and bigger and be reminded every minute until the baby was born of what we lost (each other for one thing and lots of other stuff having to do with being a kid). I barfed again.

"You have to clean that up, amigo. Got it?" Mr. Nussbaum said.

I nodded.

And then slowly life began all over.

CHAPTER 32

I 'm a keeper (Mr. Nussbaum says so).

I haven't actually seen Maggie Corrigan since the day I got yanked in my bear slippers down the hall by Mrs. Schoebel and Coach Johnson. Maggie and her mom had a final blowout that night (bad physical confrontation) because Maggie had run to my house instead of getting picked up after school by Mary. I had been hiding in the hallway and hadn't answered the door, which probably helped send Maggie over the edge with her mom (although that time was coming anyway).

No more school for Maggie. No more Bluffton either. She's gone.

The baby is being adopted by two Oberlin English professors with patches on their elbows. They're friends of the Corrigans. So Maggie is in Ohio, close to those professors, staying with her grandma while she finishes the pregnancy. The professors go to all the doctor appointments and birth classes with her, and I guess they cry and hug a lot…for joy, which I would too if I were them.

I know all this because Maggie emailed me several times over the course of a couple months. She said she is taking GED classes, and she's getting along better with her mom now that they aren't living in the same house. I thanked Maggie for the information, but I always ended my emails asking her not to contact me anymore because I worry I have a Maggie addiction like Darius has for booze.

In her last email, she talked about going to a Cleveland Cavaliers game and seeing LeBron James play and about going to huge malls with her cousin. "It's so much better in Cleveland!"

Then she stopped emailing. Like I had asked. But I haven't stopped missing her because I'm a junkie, I think. I love her.

Still, this is the best day ever—first because we're alive and second because the professors are over the moon about the baby. They can afford granola and organic macaroni and cheese and Go-Gurt for our little kid.

There are also other things to think about. So much happened so fast. With the money we got, Darius paid his fine and went to rehab. He hasn't had a drink in seventy-one days. He smiles at me when Nussbaum and I visit him in Tellurian. He sits up straight too instead of looking like a deflated balloon all the time. He apologizes for all the harm he caused me because that's part of the program. I apologize for the harm I've caused him. He hugs me back when I hug him. He hugs me like he actually cares. It's kind of like having a bit of my mom back. It's like having a real family.

Nussbaum tells me not to get my hopes up, that the booze business isn't easy to leave behind. But Darius is working hard at life, so I hope (a lot) that he can stay clean.

And things go on and on, dingles. Stuff just keeps happening all the time.

At the beginning of February, I performed in the musical. Mr. Lecroy wanted to give me back my part as Mayor of Munchkinland, but I had to refuse. This freshman, Charlie O'Neill, had been practicing at it for weeks as the understudy, and it didn't seem right for me just to boot him out the door. He sings a shitload better than I do, but he doesn't have the same pep in his cucumber or the general flash. The schedule worked better for me anyway. As a chorus munchkin and badass flying monkey, I could still go two weekdays to Nussbaum's. If I booted Charlie O'Neill, I would've had to be up at school for every practice.

Nussbaum twisted my dad's arm enough that he came down for the last show. Miz came too. They both said that I was a kick-ass monkey but that I looked a little uncomfortable as a munchkin. (I couldn't find my knee pads that night.)

Really, Nussbaum got Dad to visit for an ulterior reason.

On Sunday, me, Nussbaum, Dad, and Miz met at Country Kitchen. Between coffee and the omelets arriving, Nussbaum laid into Dad.

"Have you noticed one of your boys is in rehab and the other could have starred on a reality show with all his drama?" Nussbaum asked.

"They make their own mistakes," Dad grunted.

"There's a reason for that," Nussbaum said. "They have no adult to tell them what to do."

"Don't tell me how to raise my kids," Dad said.

"You don't raise them at all. Never did as far as I can tell. Sounds like their mother did all the work, and you hit the road as soon as she bought the farm."

"I got laid off, goddamn it. I had to go where the money was."

"Darius tells me you stopped sending money. Still, he almost managed to keep the boat floating on his own. You don't think you could've made ends meet if you'd stayed in town, gotten a little help from Darius?"

"No," Dad said.

"I call bullshit, Chuck. You weren't chasing money. You were running away."

"You back off," Dad said quietly.

"I will not, Chuck. Grow a pair and look in the mirror."

Dad looked down at the table. His chin began to tremble.

Dingus, I'd never seen my dad cry. But this was real. He swallowed hard and said, "Michelle was everything. We…we were in love since middle school, and I never, never knew what to do. But she always did. She always did right. Before she died, she told me to get my head out of my ass, but I couldn't do it. I just couldn't live in this town with these boys that reminded me of her every damn minute of the day."

Whoa. My dad ran away because I reminded him of Mom? That's not okay. While I can understand the sentiment, that's not what it means to be a dad at all. "Not okay," I mumbled.

"No," Dad said. "I know."

"I'd like Taco and Darius to move in with me," Nussbaum said. "If they'll agree to it."

I turned and looked at Nussbaum, who sat next to me. This was the first I'd heard of the plan. "Yes," I said. "I agree."

Nussbaum smiled at me then turned back to Dad. "I'd like you to send me $500 a month to keep them in food and clothes."

"Aw shit," Dad said. "I don't know."

Miz, who had been sitting quietly next to him the

whole time, just about leapt out of her skin at that point. "Goddamn it, Chuck! Of course. Of course you will send that money."

Dad looked at me so sad, dingus. He nodded. "Of course. I don't know what the hell's wrong with me. I'm sorry, Will," Dad said. "I love you, Taco, but I don't know how to do it right."

"It's okay," I said. I really don't think it's okay, but I'm not going to let my dad ruin my whole life because I can't stop being pissed at him.

Now I live in Nussbaum's little girl's room. She was so cute. There's a great photo of her and her mom on the wall. They're at the beach. I love that photo.

Nussbaum made me quit the hospital. Mallory, Nussbaum's old assistant, decided not to come back to work, so I do her whole job in half the time it took her. I am the majesty of the law. I get paid fifteen dollars an hour, which Nussbaum still says saves him mad stacks of cash over what he paid Mallory for not working very hard.

He needs that extra money. He has to pay for an expanded cable package and Netflix because he doesn't hang out at the VFW anymore. After we're done working and I get my homework finished, Nussbaum and I watch sports and movies and television from all over the globe.

Lots of times we eat Steve's Pizza or subs from Pickle Barrel. We eat so much cheese that old Nussbaum has started getting up early to get on a treadmill before he drives me to school.

Nussbaum. Yeah.

I guess there's just one last thing to tell you.

In March, I ran over to Piggly Wiggly to pick up some nondairy creamer for our coffee machine because Nussbaum had a client who was lactose intolerant. Nussbaum believes in service. "That's why I'm loaded," he says. "Because I get the people what they want so they come back again and again." So I had to run like a gazelle to buy it.

I burst in the automatic doors and waved at Sharma. (He was working a cashier line). Then I shot down the baking aisle to cut to the back. That's where I ran smack into old Dr. Patches himself, Reggie Corrigan, right in the spot where he'd tried to throw me into the mayo jars by throttling my jean jacket just nine months earlier.

"Taco!" he said, startled. "What are you sprinting through here for? Are you on the lam?"

"What lamb?" I asked. "I'm looking for nondairy creamer."

He stood back and blinked. Then he said, "Are you doing well? We saw you in the musical. You looked good."

"Yeah, I'm good. And…and how are you, sir?" I asked. My heart pounded in my shirt, my mouth went dry.

"Well, we're doing fine. It's going to be quiet, you know? Mary's packing to move overseas, and with Maggie gone…"

"Yeah, Maggie," I said. "She's pretty noisy, right?"

There was this pause. Mr. Corrigan stared at me. His mouth sort of hung open in that beard of his.

"So…I'm kind of in a hurry," I said. "Client is waiting for cream."

Mr. Corrigan sighed. He shook his head. "Can I say something?" he asked.

I shrugged.

"I'll be quick about it."

"Shoot," I said quietly.

"I want you to know I always liked you, Taco. I always thought you were doing the best you could. I don't think you're a criminal or…or poisonous."

"I know I can be a dumb kid. But I'm growing up," I said.

"You're not a dumb kid. You're a really, really good kid," he said. His face started to go red, and that made my face go red. You know how I feel about Mr. Corrigan, Dr. Patches, the man, right? He's top shelf. "I *know* that," he said.

"Thanks, sir. I appreciate it. I didn't mean to cause all this trouble. My mom told me to wait. To be the gem I am. But it's hard. I can't tell you how much—"

"Listen, Maggie was going to get in trouble with or without you, Taco. She's hardwired like that."

"She's also wired to be great and luminous. She's a bright light."

Mr. Corrigan paused and took a deep breath. "You're right. She's luminous."

Neither of us said anything. I started to feel really awkward, and I'm not the type to get awkward, dingus. So even though Nussbaum told me not to mention it ever again under any circumstances, I blurted out, "Thank you for the money, okay? You probably saved Darius's life. He paid back all the Taco Bell damage, and he's in rehab up in Madison. He's doing so well."

Mr. Corrigan looked so confused. "Rehab? We don't have that kind of money. We didn't...we didn't give you that money, Taco. When we met with Nussbaum, he said no money was necessary. After your arrest and suspension from school and... He said we didn't need to give you a cent, Taco."

"What?" I asked. My monkey brain was spinning, trying to understand how that was possible.

"I think that lawyer of yours must've—"

"Oh my Jesus," I said slowly. "Nussbaum? The money came from Nussbaum? I think I really do love Nussbaum."

I could tell you about how I confronted Nussbaum later at his office, how he cried and said he didn't want me to ever feel indebted, that he never thought he'd have a family again and now he did, but I won't, dingus. Just imagine the beauty of that sweaty old Mr. Nussbaum weeping at his desk.

Okay. I have to go now. Sharma, Emily, Brad, and I are starting a punk cello, clarinet, keyboard band. I'm the lead singer. I don't sing that great, but I've got some serious monkey magnetism. We'll likely go on tour in the next year or two, so look for us.

I'm also totally acing English, but Mr. Edwards no longer thinks I'm a math guy. He told me this during our parent-teacher conference. (Nussbaum drew the line at going, so I went in to meet with my teachers myself as if I was my own dad.) I told Mr. Edwards, "You try having two jobs and a pregnant girlfriend while learning calc!"

He said, "How about you try for a B? Make school a priority the rest of the year?"

I said, "You're on!"

He said, "Brad and Sharma will help you out, right? If they can't, just meet me during your independent study."

And I said…

Jesus. I really have to go.

Okay, here goes. And my baby?

Every day I think of you, baby.

You are going to be so smart and so funny, and your parents aren't going to believe how awesome and athletic and pretty and hilarious you are. I mean, so funny!

Your parents are going to cry happy tears every day because you are the greatest thing in the universe!

And even though Maggie and I aren't there with you in person, we are always there with you just out of sight—just the way my mom is here with me.

We love you, and your parents love you. And we are so happy your parents are happy and will do everything to make you happy.

But even if you're sad…today is the best day ever, right? So is tomorrow.

Take care, dingus. You have a good heart.

ACKNOWLEDGMENTS

Thanks to my fantastic agent, Jim McCarthy; to my supersmart editor, Annette Pollert-Morgan; and to everybody at Sourcebooks for their wonderful support. Thanks to Minnesota State University, Mankato for encouraging great writing. Thanks to my mom, Donna Herbach, who taught high school English for thirty years. Thanks to my wife, Steph Wilbur Ash, because she's hilarious. Thanks to the kids who are still funny, but who are getting too old, and so they make me sad: Leo, Mira, Christian, and Charlie. Special thanks to the students of Lancaster High School, Lancaster, Wisconsin, for helping me locate the proper restaurant.

ABOUT THE AUTHOR

Wisconsin native Geoff Herbach wanted to play for the Green Bay Packers or join the Three Stooges. His tight hamstrings prevented both pro sports and serious slapstick. Now he writes YA novels, including the award-winning Stupid Fast series and *Gabe Johnson Takes Over*. He teaches creative writing in the MFA program at Minnesota State, Mankato. Visit geoffherbach.com for more information about the author, his books, and much more.